C

MW01139567

by
Christopher Cartwright

Chapter One

Vernazza Harbor, Italy – Present Day
Seventy-Two Hours

The falling moon on the horizon shone on the only other ship in the harbor.

Its silhouette lit up against the backdrop of the medieval harbor as it drifted lazily against the natural stone breakwater. The steel ship was covered in rust. It was roughly eighty feet long with a beam of forty-five. The hull showed the outline of a fishing boat, but its rigging had long ago been removed, and its decking was now a jumbled mass of dilapidated steel. It formed a jarring contrast to the pastel colored tower homes and terraced vineyards surrounding the natural harbor along the coast of Cinque Terra.

There was no name on the vessel.

No running lights and no sound of a diesel engine running quietly. The ghost ship appeared to have just drifted into the medieval harbor, blown there by the southerly winds of the Tyrrhenian Sea or the currents of the Mediterranean Sea.

Less than fifty yards away, a man on a small wooden rowboat opened his eyes. His head hurt. He felt disoriented and hungover. He tried to blink away the haze in his memory as he searched his environment. There were pastel covered buildings in the distance, a row of colorful rowboats tied up along a jetty leading to a small sandy beach. A church tower watched over the harbor and to the other side, a masonry spiral tower, the last remnants of a medieval fortress.

None of it helped the man identify where he was or how he'd gotten there.

His head throbbed.

What the hell did I drink last night?

He touched his forehead with the palm of his left hand. There was something wet there. He blinked again. Licked his lips. It left a distinctly metallic taste in his mouth.

He frowned.

For the first time he took stock of himself.

There was blood on his face. His shirt. His arms.

He tried to swallow down the fear that was rising in his throat like bile. His head pounded with the thrum of his heart.

Where was he bleeding from?

He tried to run his hands over his body, frantically searching for the source of the blood. It was the first time he realized he was holding something in his right hand. A suitcase. That seemed odd. He made a mental note to investigate that as soon as he'd found the source of blood and managed to stem the bleeding.

After firmly patting himself down, he discovered the blood wasn't his.

It couldn't have been. If he'd lost that much blood, he would have been dead. No doubt about it. Still, the question remained, if it wasn't his, then whose was it?

His chest tightened. He sat up in the rowboat, his legs knocking something in the dark as he did. He felt around in the darkness, before gripping something. It was solid, yet supple against his grip. That alarm in the back of his head started to hammer. Something wasn't right. He traced the object down, using his hands, and came to a foot enclosed in a delicate shoe.

The person's leg was cold and wet.

He squinted as his hands fumbled around the bottom of the rowboat. A strong scent of blood intermingled with seawater filled his nostrils and he imagined the grizzly sight beneath the shroud of darkness.

He took his hands away with revulsion.

It was a dead woman. No way was she still alive.

The rowboat turned with a light breeze. Moonlight suddenly shone on the woman's face. A shiver of ice ran through his veins. She looked like an angel, with porcelain white skin, silver eyes, and brown hair. A pang of sadness touched him. The woman would have been quite beautiful at some time – before she had been murdered.

To the side of her forehead were two execution style bullet wounds.

He tried to bite down on the rising panic.

He needed to get off the water.

Whatever event led him to be where he was would have to wait. His more pressing need was to escape before someone linked him to the death of the young woman and get away from whoever killed her. Worse yet, he wondered whether he could have possibly been involved in her death.

A thick grimace developed across his face. The thought was too repugnant to accept. What had gone wrong? What sort of man might do this to a woman? His mind drifted steadily into a darker location; to answers that only the worst of people might one day stray.

The thought was tortuous, but he forced himself to ask the question.

Am I that sort of man?

He gritted his teeth. There would be no time to find out if someone caught him where he was. No, he needed to get out of there.

He searched for something to use to row with.

There were no oars.

He considered diving into the water to swim to the shore, but the sight of someone swimming in the harbor in the middle of the night might draw attention to himself. The breeze was slowly pushing him toward the beach.

He held his breath.

Anyone watching him from the harborside would merely see a man on a rowboat. That would be safer than making a swim for it. It sure didn't feel safer, but it was.

He waited.

It would only take another few minutes.

He took stock of his position. He had no idea who he was, where he had come from, or why he was sitting in a rowboat with a dead – no, not just dead – *murdered* woman in some sort of medieval harbor. He had a suitcase, the contents of which he had no idea. Otherwise he was carrying nothing. He searched for a wallet or a cell phone – anything that might reveal some indication of who he was.

His hands stopped at a small metal handle, stashed in the groove beneath his shirt, in his lower back. He retrieved it.

And sighed heavily.

It was a Russian built Makarov semiautomatic handgun. Although how he knew that at a glance, he was terrified to find out.

Working on instincts, he opened the chamber and removed the magazine – there were two rounds missing.

"Good God!" He said out loud, his voice aghast with revulsion. "I killed her!"

The wooden rowboat stopped as its bow struck the sandy beach and sank into the shore.

He inserted the magazine into the chamber and stashed the weapon behind his back again. He reached down, picked up the suitcase again, stepped off the boat…

And froze.

A chill of fear passed over him like a shadow.

From the church, a priest fixed a powerful flashlight straight on him, and yelled, "Stop! In the name of God!"

Chapter Two

Andre Dufort's eyes narrowed as he studied the man.

The man in the boat didn't seem like a killer. He looked frightened and confused. Much less certain and confident than Dufort had been led to believe. For a moment he wondered whether or not he had the right man, but it was a small doubt. After all, no one would be rowing at three in the morning. Besides, he wasn't paid to ask questions, he was paid to provide a service, for which he was uniquely qualified.

The stranger seemed trapped and panicked – making sudden and jarring movements. At this rate, the man would be lucky to reach the beach without falling in.

In contrast, Dufort was slow and precise with his movements. He had dark hair, kept well groomed, and a trim salt and pepper beard. He had a strong jaw, and defiant gray eyes. His skin was dark with a decidedly European appearance. He opened his carry bag and went through the purposeful movements of putting together the equipment of his trade.

He was perched on the crumbling rampart of the medieval castle, *Castello di Vernazza,* and had a clear view of the entire harbor. He stared through the scope of his Barrett Model 98B sniper rifle and tracked the man. The wind blew the small wooden rowboat to the shore, where the man quickly scrambled out.

Into his radio, Dufort ordered his team to wait until they had a clean shot at the man – or better yet, were in a position to take him in.

A moment later, a priest stepped out of the *Santa Margherita d'Antiochia* and, having spotted the woman's body and the blood, had determined to challenge the man.

Spooked, the man froze for an instant, and then turned to run.

Dufort shouted into his mike, "He's on the move! Take him out!"

He squeezed the trigger, sending a .338 Lapua Magnum round down the barrel at a speed of 3100 feet per second. The shot struck the sand directly behind the running man, sending an explosive spray of sand skyward.

A second shot fired before Dufort had the chance to squeeze the trigger again. It was from another sniper rifle. The shot had gone wide by about six feet, meaning that the owner either was a poor marksman or really far away.

The question was, who even knew he was there, let alone wanted to take a shot at him? The thought was unsettling.

Dufort still had a job to do.

He shifted his aim and fired a second round, but the man was already gone.

Chapter Three

He heard the snap of a rifle shot.

In a fraction of a second, his mind tried to compute all the information coming in and make a decision on his next move, concentrating on the most important questions. Where had the shot fired from? Who fired it? It wasn't the priest. That was one thing. It wasn't much, but it was all he had to go on. There was no one else in sight across the harbor, toward the church, that placed his shooter from the opposite direction – most likely somewhere up on the ramparts of the old castle.

It wasn't a lot to work with, but it was enough to act on before the next shot fired, which came almost an instant later – only this one came from the opposite direction, and unlike the first shot, which had nearly struck him, this one had obviously passed way over his head.

He ducked behind the safety of the multi-colored pastel terraces and started to run east, uphill along *Via Visconti* into the heart of the small coastal village.

He slowed for a moment to catch his breath. He was still holding the suitcase in his right hand. It suddenly seemed to stand out to him. It wasn't leather. Instead it was metallic, kind of giving him the impression of the nuclear football – the same sort of thing someone carried around with the US president.

Suddenly he felt the need to get rid of it, as though the case somehow marked him as being a wanted man.

But he couldn't do that.

Not yet anyway.

The question remained, what was so valuable inside that his hand had been practically locked onto its handle since he woke up?

Would it incriminate or exonerate him?

Fear rose in his throat. He knew he needed to do something. He couldn't go on carrying the damned thing while he was being hunted. But neither did he want to get rid of it permanently. Somewhere at some stage – if he survived the next few hours – he would need to come back and retrieve it. He felt certain that somewhere, hidden inside, were the answers he needed to find from his past – whatever they might be, he wanted to know.

Still, for the time being, he would need to stash the case.

It wouldn't take the priest very long to notify the police, and once they had found the body in the rowboat, a massive search would be underway.

His eyes swept the rows of pastel colored tower houses that lined *Via Visconti* for a place to hide it. He traced the buildings and cobbled street with his eyes, before landing on the drain way. It was roughly the size of the suitcase. He might be able to slip it inside and then retrieve it later. He bent down to examine the opening. It would probably work, but he dismissed the idea almost as soon as he had it. The fact was, if he'd had that thought, so too, would anyone else who had gone in search of it.

And someone would know the truth about his past, even if he didn't.

No. He needed a better hiding spot.

But where?

He kept moving, his gaze raking the landscape for somewhere to hide the case.

About two hundred yards along *Via Visconti* he stopped.

There was a small gap between a bright yellow tower house and a teal one. It was barely wide enough to reach into, and far too narrow to squeeze through. About twelve feet up, a horizontal drainpipe blocked one's vision of the space above.

It was the sort of hiding in plain sight that appealed to him.

He looked up and considered how to reach it.

Taking a deep breath, he stuck his left foot into the gap and tried to stand up. His foothold held. He then slid his left hand into the gap, before rotating it sideways and making a fist. It formed an iron tight wedge in the gap, the same way a rock climber might climb the crack in a mountain.

He placed his other foot higher up on the wall and shifted his weight to it. There was still the problem of moving up while holding onto the suitcase. He tentatively placed it in the crux beneath his chin and his chest. With his now free hand, he reached up and climbed higher by locking that hand into the gap, the same way he had done for the first.

Stopping just below the water pipe, he gripped the handle of the suitcase again and slid it onto the horizontal drainpipe.

The suitcase was clearly visible side on, but he doubted it could be seen from below.

He didn't wait to find out. He climbed down. A cursory glance upward revealed nothing more than a gap between two tower houses and an almost horizontal pipe.

He grinned.

It was the first bit of luck he'd had all day.

He turned to keep running east.

The man reached *Via Roma* – roughly three hundred feet away – before two Italian police officers shouted, "Fermare! Polizia!"

In the back of his mind, he realized that he must have been in Italy. It was a small detail, but he felt pitifully grateful to have something at last to grasp onto.

The men hadn't drawn their weapons, which told him that it wasn't the police who had taken a shot at him. Even so, they would as soon as they found the dead body, which would happen only minutes after they apprehended him – so that wasn't an option.

He turned and ran toward the harbor.

The police officers were older and overweight. They shouted at him, and immediately attempted to pursue him. He heard the thump of their heavy boots echoing between the narrow confines of the cobbled stone street – but they were no match for his speed.

His heart pounded.

At the end of the street he reached the harbor. His glance darted toward the rowboat. It was pulled up on the beach, and under the faint glow of a streetlight, revealed the grizzly mess of his past for all to see – possibly even the evidence needed to convict him of the murder he couldn't remember.

The priest stared at him and pointed. "He's over there!"

The man turned left and followed a narrow set of masonry stairways that hugged the natural rocky harbor, meandering upward and around the elegant buildings that lined it. The trail narrowed as he climbed toward the point.

He passed an open door, leading into the rocky face of the harbor.

Something in the deep subconscious part of his brain told him there was something wrong with an open door at this time in the morning. People are at home in bed during the dead of night, or if they were working, they would be moving – but no one would leave a door open.

The man's ears pricked up.

Someone was following him. He darted into a small lookout dug into the mountainside. It was an enclosed section of a rock that overlooked the sea. He stepped inside.

And was greeted by two men with guns.

Neither looked like police officers.

If he had to guess – which he did – these were paid goons, sent to fetch him.

One of the men fixed a pistol on him. "All right, that will do now. You're done running…"

He twisted the palms of his hands skyward. "All right, all right. I'll stop. Just tell me what I've done?"

The second one opened a butterfly knife. "And you're not here to ask questions. I'm afraid you're here to answer what we want to know."

Chapter Four

His heart pounded in the back of his head.

He pursed his lips and breathed hard, still trying to catch his breath from the constant uphill running. He took in the two men at a glance, sizing them up for a fight, like a professional boxer might before entering the ring.

The man was no longer frightened. The reign of fear and confusion was replaced by mechanical automation as his instincts took over.

Am I a professional fighter?

The man with the knife approached him.

The man with the pistol kept it fixed on him. "Don't do anything stupid!"

His heart thumped.

The man came close to him with the knife. "Who else knows?"

He frowned, no recollection of his past having yet returned. "Knows what?"

The goon shifted the knife and it sliced him lightly beneath his shirt on his chest. It stung, but he was determined not to betray his pain.

"I'm afraid I really don't know anything. In fact, I've lost my memory. I have no idea who I am, or what I did. So, I guess we're both shit out of luck…"

The enforcer raised an eyebrow. "How stupid do you think we are?"

He shrugged. "I have no idea. I can't say whether I've ever met you or not – and if so, if you were dumb or smart."

"You've got to be kidding me." The man changed the grip of the knife so the blade tilted inward. "Look. We're going to kill you anyway. You know that. We know that. The decision here is rather simple. Do you want to die quickly, or pleading for mercy?"

He sighed and took a deep breath. "Look. I don't know. Like I said, I've lost my memory, so I have no idea whether I'm the sort of guy who would like to go out quickly and quietly, or am I the sort of guy who would like to go out against the odds writhing in pain?"

Knifeman started to laugh. "You know... you of all people, I wouldn't expect to have a sense of humor. Not after the sort of life you've led. Not after what you've done. Now what's it going to be?"

He shrugged. "I don't know. Seriously. I guess you'd better help me decide."

A third person entered the visitor's lookout and closed a thick wooden door behind him. The new arrival was decidedly shorter than the other two. He wore an expensive suit, was well groomed, and looked like a high-profile lawyer. But instead of carrying a suitcase, he carried a duffel bag. There was no doubt in his mind it contained a precision rifle and not the man's luggage.

The new arrival glanced at the two thugs. "Did he tell you?"

"Not yet, boss."

The boss turned to face him. "Well? Where did you put the suitcase?"

He shrugged. "What suitcase?"

The boss punched him hard in the gut.

It made him crouch over. The pain in his diaphragm made it impossible to breathe for a few seconds.

He slowly straightened himself up. "Ah, that suitcase."

The boss said, "You're a real asshole, you know that?"

He nodded. "I didn't know that, but your friends are trying their best to remind me."

The boss's eyes narrowed. "What is this, a joke? You think all this is funny?"

Knifeman said, "He keeps telling us he's lost his memory."

The boss frowned. "Did you try to remind him?"

"Yeah, yeah... I told him I could kill him quickly, or I could make him suffer and beg for his life."

"So, what did he say?"

Knifeman shrugged. "He said he'd lost his memory, so didn't know if he was the sort of man who wanted to go silently and painlessly in the night, or kicking and screaming in pain."

The boss gestured toward him. "So remind him!"

He took a deep breath and patiently waited until knifeman moved in close with a sharp jab of his knife.

The knife approached his chest.

He moved on instinct. His attacker had expected him to move backward.

Instead he shifted his weight to his left foot and drove his right knee up into his attacker's groin.

Knifeman cried out in agony, and the blade slipped past his left arm.

He twisted the attacker's wrist and removed the knife in one swift movement. He rotated the angle of the blade and drove it into the man's chest.

Knifeman cried out.

He rotated the blade and drove it upward. The razor-sharp blade slid effortlessly between the intercostal space, between the fourth and fifth rib, piercing the heart.

The man didn't die instantly.

He shuddered and thrashed around, like a wounded animal.

The boss yelled, "Shoot him!"

The second goon raised his pistol.

He grabbed hold of knifeman who was now struggling to breathe. There was frothy blood gurgling from his mouth.

The second goon fired a couple shots.

He swung knifeman round, using him as a human shield.

The bullets took him in the chest.

By the third shot, the man stopped moving.

He retrieved the Russian built Makarov semiautomatic handgun from where it sat in the slight groove in his lower back.

Without thinking, he returned fire – sending two shots in immediate procession at the shooter. It wasn't a conscious decision. He didn't concentrate. Or aim. Or even think. He just did. The muscle memory in his arms took over.

In a split second it was all over.

The shooter had two neat bullet wounds to the forehead. Similar to the ones he'd seen on the poor woman in the rowboat earlier.

He turned to the third man – the boss.

But the boss – realizing that they were losing the battle – had already stepped out of the building, and yelled, "Polizia! Polizia! He's up here!"

He didn't wait for them.

Instead he stepped out onto the stone pathway that hugged the point of the medieval harbor and kept running.

He reached the end of the trail and stopped. It was a ledge overlooking the sea, some fifty feet below. He glanced up at the medieval castle rampart. If he was a sniper that's where he would have positioned himself. And if the sniper was still there, he'd just entered into the man's sights.

He turned to face the polizia who yelled at him to stop.

Their weapons were drawn now.

He frowned. End of the road. He was breathing heavy from the fighting and the running. His wrist hurt from where he'd grabbed the knife, and then killed two people with expert and merciless proficiency.

What sort of man am I?

His eyes darted from the polizia, to the medieval rampart, and then over the edge.

It was about a fifty-foot drop to the sea below.

White water formed where the otherwise gentle swell had collided with the rocky shore. It was dark and difficult to see whether the water was deep or shallow. In all likelihood, the place was riddled with sharp rocks that would slice him to pieces as soon as he struck them. If he survived the jump, it would be difficult for anyone to track him.

He contemplated jumping, but didn't even know if he'd survive the impact. Worse yet, he didn't even know if he was capable of swimming. If he'd learned to swim, chances were that the muscle memory, like those that allowed him to disassemble a handgun, would kick in once he hit the water. Of course, none of that would matter if he'd never taken the opportunity to learn to swim as a child. Everyone learned to swim? He suddenly felt uncertain about that fact.

Am I the sort of person willing to risk everything on luck?

He didn't think so. Not with those type of odds. Better to take his chance with the police and a murder trial than almost certain suicide. He turned, ready to give himself up to the polizia, raising his hands upward in submission.

And the sniper began firing at him.

Presented with an impossible choice, the man accepted his fate, turned toward the ledge – and jumped.

Chapter Five

The free fall seemed longer than he expected.

He waited for his back to burn with the pain of bullets ripping through his skin. He dropped feet first all the way to the black water below.

The water jarred him, like landing on concrete from a great height. The surface-tension broke, and he dipped into the deep water below.

His entire body stung with the pain of the impact.

His feet hurt and chest throbbed – but he was alive, and that was all that mattered.

He opened his eyes.

The saltwater stung at his eyes, but he could make out the hazy blur of light coming from the surface – nothing more – but it was enough. He kicked with his legs and swam with his arms, all the time promising himself that he wouldn't stop until he reached the surface and was able to take a breath.

After what was probably only a few seconds, his head broached the surface.

He took a couple quick, deep breaths.

Before his ears filled with the rat-a-tat-tat sound of machine gun fire. The surface nearby became sprayed with bullets, sending small jets of water shooting upward.

He took one more quick gulp of air and dived downward. He reached a depth of eight or nine feet and began to swim horizontally outward, into deep water. Bullets whizzed past him – their velocity immediately stunted by the friction of the water.

He held his breath and swam as long as he could. When his chest burned so hard that another second would have forced him to take a breath underwater, he finally allowed himself to surface with a gasp.

He glanced around.

He'd probably swum fifty or more yards out.

The towering rocky peak that formed the point to the natural harbor now formed a sinister shadow, where it had blocked the moonlight from reaching him. The water was dark and his head made only the smallest streak on the landscape, allowing him to blend in with the swell coming off the harbor's point.

In the distance, he heard the report of more shots being fired, but none of them landed anywhere near him. If he had to guess, the sniper didn't know where he was. Instead, the sniper was merely firing random shots into the water to keep him scared – because frightened people make mistakes.

The shots soon went silent, replaced with the sound of shouting and recriminations.

His head whirled with a thousand questions. Was the sniper connected to the police? Or was he working on his own? Had his execution been sanctioned by the government or not? If so, which one? Was he the hero in this thriller or was he the culprit? Maybe he deserved to die? The people who had tried to hold him prisoner certainly thought so.

Am I a good person?

He didn't linger on the thought. There was time to work out all of it. But he'd never get to find answers if he was caught or killed beforehand.

He took another deep breath and swam beneath the surface, heading out around the point of the harbor. He reached the point, and headed south, back into a small alcove-like bay on the southern side of the Mediterranean village.

More than eighty feet below the vibrant houses of Vernazza, he cast a small outline on the dark beach, but in a few hours the sun would rise and the place would be searched until he or his body was found.

He considered following the coast, but there didn't seem like there were too many places to hide if he needed to along the way. The city looked like it was more of an outcrop along a coast filled with terraced olive groves and vineyards.

His eyes narrowed and he thought about which way to go. He stared at the houses perched more than eighty feet above him, overlooking the cliff. If he could get there, he might find somewhere to hide for a few days until things settled down. Maybe the polizia might even assume he'd died in the sea.

He turned his gaze to the cliff face.

There was something familiar about the sight. He had the uncanny, and vivid feeling of déjà vu. More than that. Maybe somewhere he'd grown up, or at least visited regularly as a child? He kept studying the landscape, searching for clues about his past. He stopped and smiled.

A small trail was etched into the jagged cliff face. As the angle of the cliff rose to vertical, the trail petered out and was replaced by a forty-foot steel ladder, which draped from the last house in the row of colorful terraces.

He was certain he'd climbed the ladder before.

But that didn't necessarily mean that he should climb it again. Even if he had visited the place as a child, how would that help him escape his current situation?

He paused for a moment, trying to rationalize whether or not to climb the ladder.

And then heard the loud thump-thump of a police search and rescue helicopter, followed by its powerful spotlight beam.

It was searching the coastal waters, but would soon return to search the shores.

He ran toward the jagged trail and climbed to the top of the vertical ladder. It brought him out onto the top of the flat roofs, which nearly touched at varying heights. He glanced over his shoulder, back at the dark swell of the sea below. The helicopter was below him now, hovering, but its tail rotor was turning, and the pilot was bringing the Eurocopter AS365 Dauphin round to commence its coastal search pattern.

He stared at the helicopter for a moment and grinned. He didn't just recognize it as a helicopter. He'd recognized it at a glance as a Eurocopter AS365 Dauphin. That sort of certainty meant only one of two things. He was either a helicopter mechanic or a pilot.

The thought gave him some hope. An hour ago, he was certain he was nothing more than a good for nothing thug. A murderer of women and heaven forbid, a possible rapist. But now, he had reason to believe he was either a pilot or a mechanic. Either option meant he was smart enough to be more than hired muscle or an enforcer to a drug cartel. But neither absolved him from the facts he knew, which included that he was carrying a Russian handgun, was being hunted by men from the Russian mafia, and had most likely killed a beautiful woman only hours earlier…

But still, it meant there was hope that he was better than all of that…

The Eurocopter banked and came around for a second run along the coast. It snapped him out of his reverie. The time for working out who he was, where he'd come from, and where he should head could all be determined later. Right now he needed to find somewhere to hunker down for a while until the heat blew over.

There was no longer any uncertainty in his mind. He needed to get out of sight and that meant he needed to get off the roof. He ran north, along the gradually descending roof tops, until he reached a blue one. This was what he was after. He knew it without hesitation, although he couldn't say why.

He dropped over the side of the roof onto a balcony that overlooked the sea more than eighty feet below. Everything about the balcony felt familiar. It had terracotta tile flooring, with a glass balustrade that was at a jarring contrast to the rest of the building, which was abundantly medieval.

He turned around and looked into the apartment. The door was open and a beaded fly screen draped from the frame. Whoever lived there clearly wasn't worried about intruders, and with the warm Mediterranean breeze, they had little use for the glass door.

His eyes glanced inside. The lights were off, but being the middle of the night, that didn't necessarily mean the place was empty. He cringed at the thought of the occupant's reactions when they woke up to find a stranger in their house.

Overhead, the Eurocopter banked to face him, its giant searchlight fixing along the rooftop. It was now or never. He swallowed hard, parted the fly screen and stepped inside.

The building shook for a few seconds under the downdraft of the Eurocopter's powerful rotor blades, before the helicopter disappeared into the distance, and he was left standing in the dark room in silence.

If someone was home they were awake now, their every sense alert and listening for the unusual sound over the otherwise silent coastal village. At worst, they would turn on the lights any moment, and find him there.

He stood still, preparing for the worst.

Where would he move to? Where could he hide? If he was spotted, would he attack them or would he run? He felt worried that he might act on impulse and kill the innocent occupant. He knew very little about himself, but one thing had been abundantly clear – if he was cornered, he would fight ruthlessly to survive.

He couldn't leave, but if he stayed, something very bad was going to happen.

Instead, he flicked on the light and tentatively said, "Hello. I'm sorry to disturb you."

He wanted to give his name, but had none to provide.

His eyes narrowed and his jaw hardened as he swept the medieval apartment. There was a small kitchenette and living room overlooking the dark sea to the south. An open door led to a bathroom. Next to it was a doorway, presumably to the outside, and a small hallway to the bedrooms.

He switched on the light in the hallway. He spoke in a gentle, soothing tone. "It's okay, I'm not here to hurt you. I just need some help."

There was no response.

He opened the first bedroom door.

It had a double bed with its sheets neatly made up, a closet with a few dresses and other summer outfits – not enough to warrant someone who permanently lived there, but more likely a vacation house – and a couple photos on a bedside table. He picked up one, and glanced at it. The photo showed a beautiful woman in Johns Hopkins University graduation robes. She had blonde hair, brown eyes, and a firm smile that appeared restrained, as though she was burdened by her newfound wealth of knowledge. She was carrying a certificate, but the name and details were blurred.

He put the photo frame back down and stepped out of the room, suddenly feeling like an intruder. He turned off the light and headed toward the second bedroom door. There was more confidence in his movement this time. He was almost certain no one was home.

Stepping into the second room, he switched on the light. "Hello. Is anyone here?"

He took in the room at a glance. As he expected, the room was empty. It was a relatively tidy study, with a cedar desk, open laptop, and assortment of various technical books. Judging by the dense technical books, he guessed she was an academic of some sort.

Other than that, he gathered very little about her or why he should so vividly recall the house she lived in.

He made his way back to the bathroom.

He ran the faucet with warm water and washed his face. He examined himself in the mirror. It seemed strange to stare at a foreign face and know that it was your own. He had thick brown hair, a dark beard, and piercing blue eyes like the ocean, which stared back at him.

The man exhaled slowly, his eyes narrow and searching. He no longer saw a man. Instead, he saw something entirely different. Like a ghost, his previous life had been erased. A dangerous man with no memory of his past.

He shook his head. "Who the hell are you?"

Chapter Six

Andre Dufort stared at the dark ocean down below.

A crispy string of white wash slithered slowly toward the jagged rocks, like a sinister creature of the sea, before it dispersed and the swell flattened to nothing.

He shook his head and frowned.

There was no way anyone could hold their breath that long. The man had either drowned, or attempted to swim farther out to sea to find another place to return to the shore. If that was the case, the police helicopters – which were already in the air – would find him. If not, the man was dead.

Andre's success was marred by a strange sense of disappointment. If his target was indeed dead, then he'd completed his job, and could walk away now without ever being implicated in the man's death. It was an easy solution. Yet, somehow it felt wrong. From what he'd read about the target, he had expected something more.

The man was meant to be extraordinary. A real challenge. He'd felt elated and thrilled by the hunt, the same way a hunter might, on the chase of an African beast in the Sahara in days long since gone by. And now he was experiencing the disappointment of the aftereffect.

He went through the process of disassembling the sniper rifle, his hands mechanically stripping the weapon that had become an extension of his body, and packing it away in its case. He returned his case to the room that he'd hired the day before. He stripped himself and had a warm shower, removing any obvious sign of gunpowder residue that might incriminate him. He took his time. There was no rush. After all, in the end, he hadn't even been responsible for his target's death. Now, all he had to do was go and confirm that the sanction had been successful.

He turned the shower off, dried himself, and got dressed in a pair of dark denim jeans, shoes, and a polo shirt. He considered a collared shirt and tie, but dismissed the idea as soon as he received it. He glanced at himself in the mirror and smiled – he looked like a professional currently on vacation, but unable to shake the persona.

He nodded to himself, happy with the effect, and stepped outside.

Andre took the meandering masonry stairwell in his stride, heading down casually to the main beach at the southern end of the Vernazza harbor.

The polizia were already setting up a cordon line.

A senior officer, with a surly face turned to greet him. "You look pretty interested in my crime scene, sir."

Andre suppressed a smile. "I'm afraid I'm more interested in finding out whether or not you've found the man's body yet?"

The officer hesitated. His eyes narrowed. "What man?"

"The man who presumably killed that young lady. The same one who jumped into the ocean and never came back up again."

"So you saw that too, did you?"

Andre nodded.

The officer said, "What else did you see?"

"Not much. I saw the man get off the rowboat on the beach there at 3:21. Someone challenged him… a priest, I think from Santa Margherita d'Antiochia – I'm afraid I couldn't see his face. I saw the murdered woman, too. Then, someone fired a shot, and the man made a run for it."

"You saw a lot," the police officer said without hiding the suspicion from his voice.

"I'm staying at an apartment, right there," Andre said, pointing up at his apartment, which had a clear view of the beach. "I could see everything from the balcony."

"What were you doing watching from your balcony at three in the morning?"

Andre held his breath for a moment. It would be interesting to see how the police officer took the next part of his story. "I was waiting for a Russian fugitive to step off a boat."

Chapter Seven

Andre watched the police officer's lips twist into a wry smile, riddled with incredulity.

Contrary to frequent portrayals in popular culture, Interpol is not a supranational law enforcement agency and has no agents who are allowed to make arrests. Instead, it is an international organization that functions as a network of criminal law enforcement agencies from different countries. Interpol's collaborative form of cooperation is useful when fighting international crime because language, and cultural and bureaucratic differences can make it difficult for police officials from different nations to work together.

"Andre Dufort. I'm a senior investigator with Interpol."

"Gabriele Valentino." The officer's eyes widened with understanding. "Chief of the Polizia for La Spezia."

Andre handed him his Interpol ID. "Pleased to meet you."

Valentino ran his eyes across the ID. His face hardened. "Do you mind telling me what Interpol knows about my crime scene, and why we weren't informed earlier… when we might have had a chance to do something about it?"

"I'm sure they would have if they knew anything in advance."

The police officer frowned. "They knew enough to send you here!"

"No. I was already here on vacation. When a tip came in that this man was going to defect, I was immediately contacted."

"Why?" The police officer asked. "It's not like you could have apprehended the man."

"No. I was purely there for reconnaissance. I got the call about five minutes too late. My superiors were hoping that he would swim ashore and that I could follow him to wherever he was going to stay for the night."

The police officer frowned. "Only he never reached his destination."

"No. Someone took a shot at him."

The police officer shook his head. "Not just someone. Two people."

"Really?" Andre arched an eyebrow. "Are you sure?"

"Yeah. Someone fired a high-powered sniper rifle, perched, presumably, on top of the remains of *Castle Doria*."

"And the other person?"

"Somewhere near the church. A priest interrupted your man on the beach, startling him, and he ran. If the priest hadn't, the man would have been killed. I find it unlikely two expert marksmen could have missed a shot like that, don't you?"

Andre nodded. "I agree. So he ran."

"Until we caught up with him – whereupon he jumped into the *Ligurian Sea*."

Andre placed his hands in his pockets, with an air of practiced casualness. "Where he never resurfaced, meaning he's most likely dead."

"That's right. But not before he killed two people."

That was news to Andre. "He killed two people?"

"Yeah. They look like hired thugs. Mercenaries or just bad people. Real tough… well, maybe not so tough after all. It looks like they threatened your man, maybe they had been sent there to kill him, I don't know. Either way, it went wrong for them, and right for your guy, who came out killing both of them."

A suppressed grin curled upward on Andre's lips. *That's more like the man I was led to believe the target to be.* "I was informed under no circumstances was I to try and apprehend him on my own. Even if I had the legal authority to do so in Italy – which I don't – I was told the man would be dangerous."

The police officer met his eyes with a hardened glare. "So, what has he done?"

Andre handed him the Interpol Red Card. "Have a read for yourself."

There are eight types of notices, seven of which are color-coded by their function: Red, Blue, Green, Yellow, Black, Orange, and Purple. The most well-known notice is the Red Notice which is the one described as the closest instrument to an international arrest warrant in use today. An eighth Special Notice is issued at the request of the United Nations Security Council.

Valentino examined the Red Card. "Your man's a cyber terrorist?"

"From what I hear."

"He seems to know how to handle himself very well for a computer hacker."

Andre shrugged. "You got the same card I have."

"Alone and trapped, he killed two thugs without much effort."

"Yeah. If he was a computer geek, it sure as hell wasn't all he was." Andre turned his gaze to the dead girl in the wooden rowboat. "What about her? Did he kill her?"

Valentino shrugged. "I don't know – yet. One of my detectives is currently taking notes on the crime scene. We'll know more shortly."

Andre stared at her lifeless body. "Do we know who she is?"

"No." Valentino sighed. "We were hoping you might be able to tell us."

Andre studied her face.

There were two execution style shots to her head. She looked young, and quite pretty once upon a time. *What a waste of a life…*

The sight brought with it a chill of fear that swept across him like a shadow. It was like seeing a ghost. None of it made sense. Nothing about this night was making sense. Anomalies weren't an unusual part of a contract like his. Normally, he just had to improvise and deal with them without adding too much collateral damage. That's what he would have to do here, but the dead woman was the worst of his anomalies to deal with. Because of her, he couldn't simply accept his target had drowned and then collect his payment.

Instead, he would need to find out how she ended up in the equation.

Andre turned to face the chief of police. "She's not familiar to me, but when your detective finishes up, if he would be so kind as to send me a copy of the photos and fingerprints, I'll send them to our team at Interpol Headquarters, back in Lyon. Hopefully someone there will be able to shed some light on the situation."

"Good, good… Vernazza is a small village, but a very popular tourist location. It would be very sad to taint it with the murder of a local woman or a tourist, going about their everyday lives."

"I understand what you're saying. If we were to discover that… for example, she was working for the Russian Mafia or something, it would be easier for you to issue a press release to that effect, giving the locals and tourists alike, a stronger feeling of safety."

"Exactly."

"I'll let you know as soon as I do, what they have on her back at Lyon." Andre turned on his flashlight and shined its beam on the dilapidated ship. "What about the boat? Does that belong there?"

"No. We've spoken to some locals. They say it wasn't there late last night, which means it drifted in around the same time as your Red Card."

"Does the ship have a name or any registration numbers?"

"No."

"Have you been on board?"

"Yes, but there was nothing obvious." Valentino nodded. "We'll still have the ship towed to La Spezia for more detailed forensic examination, but so far, it looks like nothing more than a rusty ship inside. If anything, it makes me doubt your man even arrived on board – unless he's been adrift for some time."

Andre smiled. "What a crime scene, hey?"

Valentino nodded. "I've never seen anything like it. A guy floats into a peaceful, medieval harbor, in the dead of night with a woman he's most likely murdered. He gets challenged by a local priest who witnesses him floating toward the beach. He then gets shot at by two snipers. Before being attacked by two thugs, who he then kills, and then when confronted by my officers, he chooses to jump onto a ledge of jagged rocks in the sea."

"Yeah, it's bizarre." Andre turned and bit his lower lip. "Do you mind?"

"What?"

He grinned. "If I take a look at your ghost ship?"

Chapter Eight

The ghost switched off the lights.

In the dark, he sat still and listened to the pandemonium outside continue. The downdraft of the search and rescue police helicopter's rotary blades thumped in the distance. The Polizia on the cobbled streets outside barked orders, cordoned off the beach, and presumably brought out forensic teams to investigate the murder of the woman in the rowboat.

He waited until the commotion settled down.

When the immediate fear of getting caught subsided, boredom crept in. He waited some more, until the gray of predawn rose on the horizon, giving him enough light to see his environment clearly. His eyes swept the room, searching for clues that might reveal something from his past.

His gaze traced the outline of the living room. It was tidy, and barely lived in. There was a small TV with a set of rabbit ears style antennae on top that looked like it was straight out of the seventies. A small refrigerator that was switched off at the power point and the door was left open, suggesting the owner had left it to air, while he or she was away. His stomach rumbled and he felt disappointed to see that the owner had obviously left for the season.

He turned to the cupboard and found an array of canned food with no expiration dates visible. For a moment, he wondered whether they had been there since he was a child – or whenever it was that he'd spent time living in the coastal apartment. He rifled behind the cans, and found a small container of oats. They looked intact. Not that he really knew what oats looked like when they were past their used by date. Next to the oats were a couple cans of condensed milk. It wasn't much in the way of taste, but his stomach assured him it would be better than nothing.

He added water to rehydrate the milk, poured some over the oats, and sat down at the boutique dining table to have breakfast, overlooking the ocean.

His lips turned upward into a grin. The vista was quite stunning as the first rays of sun danced on the surface of the sea, flickering like diamonds. Something about the sight caught his attention. The familiarity of it was as breathtaking as the landscape was beautiful. It began to put him at ease for the first time since he'd woken up on the rowboat without his memory.

He slowly ate his breakfast.

And a moment later, he heard the soft sound of a key being inserted into a lock, and turned without hesitation.

He turned to find somewhere to hide, but the only potential places were past the now opening door.

He tried to set his lips with a disarming smile.

Maybe there was still a chance he could talk his way out of this. He kept holding the bowl and spoon in front of him, in the hope that no one who was really dangerous, would break into someone's house only to steal breakfast cereal.

An instant later, the door opened, and a beautiful woman walked through.

She was the one from the photograph he'd examined earlier. A Johns Hopkins University graduate. She had aged about fifteen or maybe even more years, but there was no mistaking it was the same person. Her skin was darkly tanned, giving her a decidedly Mediterranean and exotic appeal. She had blonde hair, brown eyes, and a kind face.

Her lips parted into a beaming smile and bewilderment. "Sam Reilly, what are you doing here?"

He opened his mouth to speak. His blue eyes filled with a mixture of fear, surprise, and relief.

She glanced at his crestfallen face, wrapped her arms around him and gave him a giant hug filled with familiarity. "I thought you were supposed to be in Holland by now?"

Chapter Nine

Sam Reilly felt a wave of relief.

Someone knew who he was. Technically, she was the second person he'd met who knew who he was, but she was the first who didn't appear to want to kill him.

"You know who I am?" he asked.

"Yes, of course... I mean, I know who you were, why?" Her appearance twisted into puzzled concern. "What are you talking about?"

He raised the palms of his hands. "I'm afraid I've lost my memory."

Her brown eyes locked with his, searching. Instead of doubt and distrust, her face was plastered with empathy and genuine concern. "You're serious, aren't you?"

Sam nodded. "Afraid so."

She hugged him again, this time holding on a little longer. They were roughly the same height. She was neither slim nor heavy. There was strength and muscle in her frame, but there was a softness to her, too. Her hair filled his nose with the scent of her shampoo, which was rich with exotic flowers. She finally pushed away, and took a seat on the sofa overlooking the ocean.

He swallowed, feeling the slight loss of an emotion when she stepped away from their embrace. Something about the sign of affection seemed familiar, as though it was teasing at some long ago and distant memories – no, not yet memories, but more feelings. It stirred once powerful feelings, emotions and desires.

He tried to blink away the haze in his memory. Frustration and loss teased at his heart, but he couldn't put any of it together. He sat down next to her. She looked at him. Her face was wrapped up in empathy, patience, and regret… buried beneath the bewilderment was some sort of suppressed smile, a type of joy, and maybe, he hoped, some desire.

She blushed, as though she knew exactly what he was thinking. "How did this happen?"

Sam shrugged. "I don't know. How would I? I've lost my memory."

Her eyes narrowed. "What's the last thing you remember?"

"I woke up in the middle of the night on a rowboat in the harbor – what harbor is this by the way?"

"Vernazza, Italy. Part of the five cities of Cinque Terra," she informed him.

He thought about that, and somewhere in the back of his mind, the name and the scenery somehow matched up with the databanks buried deep in his brain. "I must have drifted into the harbor. I don't know where I came from or why I was there in the first place. But ever since I reached the beach, someone's been trying to kill me."

"Someone's trying to kill you?"

Sam nodded. "It would appear so."

"Who?"

"To be honest, I think the question so far is, who isn't trying to kill me? Let me see, I reached the beach and was stopped by a priest. When I looked up to reply to him, I was shot at by two separate people."

"Two people? Maybe it was just the same person taking multiple shots?"

"No. It was two separate shooters. Snipers, positioned high up on opposing positions within the harbor. I could tell because of the way the .338 Lapua Magnum shot made a crisp report, distinct to the rimless, bottlenecked, centerfire rifle cartridges."

She grinned. "You could tell all that by the echo of the shots?"

Sam paused, only just then realizing the oddity in knowing such complex information at the blink of an eye, or in this case, the snap of a sniper shot. "I guess so."

"Can you normally tell things like that about weapons being fired?"

Sam bit his lower lip and smiled. "I don't know. You'd better tell me. Am I the sort of person who knows enough about weapons to instinctively tell you what sort of weapon was fired?"

She shook her head. "No. I don't think so. I mean, you weren't the last time I saw you."

"How long ago was that?" Sam asked.

She paused, thought about it for a moment, and said, "I'd say nearly fifteen years."

"That's nearly a lifetime ago. Almost half my life time…" Sam glanced at himself in the reflection of the window. "How old am I?"

"You're thirty-eight."

He mulled that over for a moment and decided he was doing okay. He didn't look young for his age, but neither did he look older than that. There were some dark creases in his face that suggested he'd seen his share of difficulties, but overall, he'd had a good life, without any major stumbling blocks with vices. His face certainly wasn't that of a heavy smoker, or drinker for that matter.

"I haven't seen you since I was twenty-three?"

"No. Twenty-four. You were born in December."

He nodded, taking it all in. "Can I ask you something?"

She squeezed his hand. There was a comfort there, a natural relationship that their bodies had that felt as though it had once been more than just a friendship. There was muscle memory in their hands, even though his brain couldn't remember a thing about her. She said, "Sure. Anything."

"What's your name?"

She took a deep breath. "Wait. Are you telling me you don't remember me at all?"

Sam winced. "I'm afraid not. Were we close?"

"Yeah, kinda…" she made a coy smile that looked like she was working hard to suppress something from her past.

Sam said, "I'm sorry."

She nodded, squeezed his hand again in a subtle gesture of acceptance. "It's okay. Not your fault. Let's start again… Hi, I'm Catarina Marcello."

Sam shook her hand, in mock formality, "Sam Reilly."

She grinned. "It's a pleasure to meet you, really it is, Mr. Reilly."

"Catarina Marcello?" Sam said the name out loud, letting it sink into his own ears, hoping that it would jog his memory somewhere. "Can I call you, Cat?"

"You asked that the first time we met!"

"What did you say?"

"I said I didn't like the name."

"What did I end up calling you?"

"Cat."

"Really?"

"Afraid so. It was a joke at first, but the name stuck."

Sam said, "Sorry."

She laughed. "Don't worry about it. The name's grown on me."

They sat there in silence, their eyes drifting out across the glistening ocean, all the way to the horizon. Neither one knowing what to say next, what to ask, or where to go from here. Sam's brain, despite having no memory, was working like a complex computer, calculating everything he'd learned, what he knew, and where he should go next.

Sam turned to face her. "You said we were close. What happened?"

"That's a long story."

"I have time… I think?"

Catarina said, "We met here on vacation."

Listening to her accent, which was a rich combination of an Italian accent mixed in with a predominantly American drawl. He tried to place its origins, deciding on somewhere Mid-Atlantic. "You're American?"

"Yes. But my dad's Italian. We immigrated to the US when I was in my early teens, but he kept his family home. I like to use it during the summer break each year. You taught me to SCUBA dive around the reef, just over there."

Sam grinned. "I can SCUBA dive?"

Catarina's lips parted in a smile, part incredulous, part bewilderment. "Yeah. You weren't too bad at it."

"What's that meant to mean? Was I a dive instructor or something?"

"No. A marine biologist, actually. To be honest, when I met you, I think you were permanently spending most of your life diving in remote and exotic locations."

"Sounds like a nice life."

"It was. I followed you in it for nearly two years. We traveled the world together and had a wonderful time."

Sam felt somber at the thought. He wished he could remember it. "What happened?"

"What do you mean?"

"If it was all so wonderful, why did we ever stop?"

"Well…" she was hesitant. "I finished my course and had to start real work, and living."

"And that was it?" Sam asked. "You mean, we went our separate ways because you had to start work? That seems a little hard to believe."

"No. There was more to it than that."

"Like what?"

She paused, swallowed. "To be honest, I asked you to marry me."

Sam glanced at her. She was intelligent, nurturing, empathetic, and painstakingly beautiful. Every nerve in his body wanted to touch her and be held close to her. He frowned. He couldn't imagine any world in which he would have turned her down.

His brow furrowed with incredulity. "I turned you down?"

"Yes."

"Why?"

Her gaze avoided him. "We were both young. You said there was more to see in the world. But that wasn't it."

"I would have loved you very much."

She smiled, her doleful brown eyes were wide, and distant, as though they were miles away. "We were smitten with each other."

Sam persisted. "So, what went wrong?"

"You joined the marines."

"Why?"

"I don't know. I think you did it to piss off your father, who tried to insist you join the family business, which as far as I could tell was to make money."

Sam didn't bother to ask what his family did. He didn't care. Right now, he just had to know what could have possibly caused him to drift away from someone like her. "And you left."

She smiled. But there was still pain in her face. "No. I would have waited for you. Whatever you wanted. I would have followed you anywhere and everywhere you wanted to go."

"I broke up with you?"

"Yeah."

"Why?"

Catarina's lips parted in a coy smile. "I'm afraid I can't answer that one."

Sam's eyes narrowed. "Can't?"

"No. That's something you're going to have to work out for yourself."

"Why?" Sam expelled a deep breath. "I couldn't imagine ever wanting to let you out of my sight, let alone break up with you. What went wrong?"

"Honestly?"

"Yeah…"

"You were so angry at me – I don't think you ever forgave me."

"Why?" he asked, feeling suddenly sad at the thought of ever quarreling with someone so lovely.

She crossed her arms. "No. I'm afraid, that's something you're going to have to remember for yourself."

Chapter Ten

Sam tried to pry the truth out of her.

His attempts fell short and he was met by Catarina's ironclad refusal to talk on the subject. He didn't persist very long. No reason to distance himself from the only lifeline he'd found since waking up.

Failing to break through her defenses, Sam's mind turned to what he knew about her so far. She was an Italian immigrant to the US, who went on to become a university graduate from a prestigious Ivy League University – Johns Hopkins University. Her parents were far from poor if they had kept their old apartment in Vernazza out of sentimental reasons for the occasional vacation. He and Catarina had dated, nearly ended up married, and then separated because something she had done had made him so angry that he had pigheadedly decided to never talk to her again.

His thinking turned to what she knew about him.

He was a marine biologist, who joined the marines to upset his dad who wanted him to join the family business, whatever that was. He used to take her SCUBA diving in exotic locations throughout the world. They hadn't spoken in more than fifteen years – yet, she knew that he was supposed to be in Holland.

Sam asked, "If we haven't spoken in fifteen years, how did you know I was meant to be in Holland?"

Catarina said, "You called me last night."

"When?"

"About eight-thirty. It was completely out of the blue."

"What did I have to say?"

"Not much. Only that you wanted to see me, and that it was really important that we talked in person – face-to-face."

Sam grinned. "And now I'm here."

"Yeah, but I have no idea why or what you wanted to talk about."

"Did we plan for a time to meet up?"

"No. Only…"

"What?"

"You said that you needed to be somewhere in Holland on the fourth. It was vitally important and you couldn't risk being late, even to speak to me…"

"Do you know where I was going in Holland?" Sam paused, realizing he was using the misnomer for the Netherlands. It was a trivial detail many people overlooked, including some Dutch people who referred to it as Holland, even though it only represented the two provinces of North and South Holland. He suddenly grinned.

She asked, "What?"

"I just remembered that Holland isn't the country's real name."

She shrugged. "Many people call it that."

"I know. I'm not being pedantic. I'm just surprised that I remembered it. The fact that it stirred some sort of hidden indignation suggests maybe I have some connection to the country. Could that be the case?"

"Not that I know of."

Sam tried to process the meaning. Failing to do so, he returned to the original question. "Do you know why I was on my way to the Netherlands?"

"No." She closed her eyes, trying to think back to the conversation. "Wait. You said you had an important meeting at The Hague!"

He arched an eyebrow. "The Hague?"

"You know, the third largest city in the Netherlands?"

"Right," Sam said, trying to picture the coastal city, but failing to have any visual memory of the place. "The area of the former County of Holland roughly coincides with the two current Dutch provinces of North Holland and South Holland in which it was divided, which together include the Netherlands' three largest cities: the de jure capital city of Amsterdam, Rotterdam, home of Europe's largest port, and the seat of government of The Hague."

Catarina said, "It's also inside the traditional region of Holland that has its roots traced back to medieval times."

"That's interesting. You think that maybe there's a connection to why I was so indignant about the use of the country's misnomer?"

She smiled. "I have no idea."

Sam asked, "Any chance I mentioned what I was supposed to be doing there?"

She shook her head. "Afraid not."

"Maybe I was sightseeing?"

"I doubt it. You sounded like whatever it was that you wanted to talk to me about was really important… I tried to talk you into coming here, but you wouldn't hear of it… you just told me that you had a meeting at The Hague on the fourth, and couldn't risk missing it."

"The fourth?" Sam frowned. "What day is it today?"

She paused, as though suddenly considering the date. "It's the first."

"Okay, so I have, what… seventy-two hours to find out what's so important in The Hague?"

"No. It's already eleven o'clock. That means you're down to sixty-one."

Sam thought about that for a moment. "So, I need to find a way to get to The Hague in the next sixty-one hours. It might be difficult without money…"

"I can lend you money for the flight," she said without hesitation.

"Thanks, but I'm not sure it will do me much good without a passport."

"No. That might be difficult. We could go down to the US embassy in Florence. We could drive there today and get you an emergency travel passport."

Sam thought about that. "They're still going to want to know how I got into the country, where I've been, and who knows what I have done since losing my memory? Besides, I don't have any form of ID. What are they to go on?"

"You sure you don't have anything? Not even a license in a pocket or something?"

"No. Nothing at all." Sam paused a beat. "Wait! When I woke up on the rowboat, I was carrying a suitcase."

"What was in it?"

"I don't know. It was locked and I didn't have time to try and break it open with all the... you know, bad guys trying to kill me and all."

"So where's the suitcase now?"

"I hid it."

"Where?"

"There's a building with a small gap between a bright yellow tower house and a teal one. It was barely wide enough to reach into, and far too narrow to squeeze through. About twelve feet up a horizontal drainpipe blocked one's vision of the space above – I stashed it up there."

"All right. I'll go get it as soon as the morning wave of tourists disappears."

"Why you and not me?"

"Because no one knows me."

"Okay, thanks." Sam grinned. "The tourists... they come in waves?"

"Yeah, the morning train drops off hundreds of tourists at Riomaggiore, where they make their way along the famous Cinque Terra coastal hike. As a result of that influx, and despite your escapades last night leading the polizia to cordon off large sections of Vernazza, there will be hundreds of tourists swarming through the town for the next few hours."

"So we have a few hours to wait."

"Afraid so."

"It's frustrating when the only thing I know is that I somehow need to be in The Hague in less than three days."

Catarina sighed. "There's nothing you can do about it. I mean, if you want you can gamble trying to get it during the peak time, but it's almost a certainty someone will spot you – and I can't say what might happen if they do."

Sam nodded. "I know. I can imagine what would happen if you were caught. With so many polizia around, you would be forced to open the suitcase, and then who knows what they would find – maybe the truth about my past, and maybe something that incriminates me."

"I doubt it. Whatever's happened, you're not a criminal."

Sam crossed his arms. "How can you be so sure?"

"Because you're not."

"What about organized crime?"

She laughed and fixed her gaze on his. "Jesus! You're serious! Why are you asking?"

"I just need to know. That's all. I was attacked by three men who I'm pretty certain were part of the Russian mafia. They said I was a bad man and my death wouldn't be missed by anyone."

"My god, how did you escape?"

Sam recalled the incident. He'd killed two of them within seconds, with the ease of a trained assassin. He swallowed. "I defended myself and ran off."

"So you're worried you might have been part of the mafia?"

"It certainly crossed my mind as a possibility." There was unexplained guilt in his voice. "After all, you should have seen how well I defended myself. I was barbaric."

She didn't recoil at his admission. "Last time I saw you, you had joined the marines. I assume you learned to defend yourself there."

"Yeah. Maybe. This seemed a little more than just basic training in hand to hand combat."

"It comes naturally to some people. You've obviously retained muscle memory from your time in the marines."

"But you're certain I didn't join the Russian mafia?"

"No way in the world."

"Why?" Sam persisted. "Is it that impossible to think that my life had changed that much in the past fifteen years?"

"Yes. I find it impossible to believe."

He met her eye. "How can you be so sure?"

"For a start, I know you…" She grimaced, slightly hurt, and looked away. "Or at least I did, once. Besides, you just simply didn't have the sort of personality that leads someone to enter the world of organized crime."

Sam said, "People change."

She shook her head emphatically. "Not that much. No one changes that much."

He turned his gaze to avoid her eyes. "There's something else you should know about me."

"What?"

Sam swallowed hard. "I'm pretty certain I murdered a girl last night."

Chapter Eleven

Sam filled her in with what he knew about finding the dead woman on the rowboat with the execution style bullet holes in her head, and the Russian built Makarov semiautomatic handgun in his pants, the fact that he instinctively knew how to disassemble the weapon – and that it was missing two rounds.

"You didn't kill that woman." Catarina's words were emphatic.

Sam arched an eyebrow. "What makes you so sure?"

"I don't know. You're not that type of person. You're bound by a stringent code of duty and honor, which would prohibit gross murder."

Sam bit his lower lip. "I may have killed two thugs – presumably Russia mafia – in self-defense earlier."

"Even so, that's self-defense."

"Maybe I killed the girl to save myself?"

She shrugged. "Maybe. It still doesn't make you a murderer."

Sam said, "Should I leave? I mean, there's no reason for you to feel unsafe in your own house."

Her gray eyes sparkled as they fixed quizzically on him. "You think I'm having second thoughts, and am worried that I've inadvertently let a murderer into my house?"

"Technically, I let myself in, but yeah... aren't you?"

"No. Not in the slightest. I'll bet my life there's a perfectly good explanation that will absolve you of all wrongdoing."

"All right. But I don't plan on staying here, burdening you, for any longer than I have to."

"Agreed." Catarina's voice turned hard. "On that subject, we need to get you to a hospital. You might have sustained a serious injury."

"No. It's okay. I feel fine… apart from the fact that I can't remember anything about my life before waking up on a rowboat this morning."

"You need to be assessed."

"I can't."

"Why not?"

Sam said, "Because I don't know what I've done or who's trying to kill me. One thing's for certain, whoever it is who's looking for me, they have powerful resources, which means they would have someone keeping an eye out at the local hospitals."

"Would they?"

Sam shrugged. "I would. A man wakes up with no memory of his life beyond the day he woke up, surely the first thing he's going to do is find a hospital and get checked out."

"And yet you won't."

"No. I can't."

Catarina smiled. "Okay, okay… you'd better let me have a look at you."

"Why?" Sam met her eye. "Are you a doctor?"

She nodded, her lips parting into a coy smile. "I am."

"What sort?"

"A medical one! Not a philosopher…"

"Why didn't you tell me before? I've still got a terrible headache, and I'm only just now feeling like the dangerous combination of drugs and alcohol that I must have taken last night, are starting to wear off."

"Well…" Catarina said, biting her lower lip. "Because you're not going to like it…"

"Why?"

"Because the coincidence is a little hard to explain. In fact, I've been struggling to find an excuse for it… or something to justify it, but to be honest, I'm at a loss."

Sam swallowed. "Good God. What sort of doctor are you?"

"I'm a neurologist."

"A brain surgeon?"

"Yes, although I haven't practiced surgery for about five years."

"Why?"

"Because I've been working on a project to map the memory databases of the human brain."

Sam exhaled slowly. "You're a leading expert on memory?"

"Afraid so," she admitted.

"That's some coincidence, huh?" Sam said, his voice level. "One day I wake up with global amnesia, this extremely rare form of complete memory loss, only to find out that I've washed ashore on a beach, right near an ex-girlfriend's place from fifteen years ago, who just so happens to be a leading expert in the field?"

Catarina grinned. "When you say it that way... yeah, what are the chances?"

Chapter Twelve

Sam's deep blue eyes locked with hers. "You didn't have anything to do with this?"

Catarina said, "No. I swear to you. This is the first time I've seen you in nearly fifteen years."

"All right."

"All right, what?"

"I believe you. It's an incredible coincidence. Maybe in some sort of subconscious way, I was searching for you to help. Hell, you even said that I tried to contact you last night, before I had lost my memory – maybe it was about whatever was going to happen to me?"

She paused. "It's a possibility. Although I can't see how you would know that you were about to lose your memory."

His eyes narrowed. "You're a memory expert, and you can't think of any way in particular this could have happened?"

"First, I'm a neurologist, specializing in memory databasing. Second, I can think of a number of ways this could have happened to you… the problem is, I've tried applying all of them to you, and none seem to make sense."

"Really? Like what?"

"The most common cause of global amnesia is severe trauma to the brain – we're talking about one hell of a concussion. But, from what I can see here, you don't have any sign of an injury to your skull."

"You can tell that just by looking at me?" Sam asked, a wry smile of incredulity forming on his lips.

"As a matter of fact, I can. Your hair is short enough that I can tell at a glance that your skull doesn't have any obvious deformities, lacerations, swelling, or bruising that suggests trauma. On a more clinical level, we know that there are certain types of bruises around the eyes called *raccoon eyes*, which are associated with a fracture at the base of the skull. Your eyes, nose, mouth, and ears aren't exuding any type of blood or clear fluid, known as CSF – that's short for cerebral spinal fluid by the way – the absence of all of this, means to me that you haven't had a significant concussion – certainly nothing likely to cause global amnesia."

"Right, what about the other possibilities?"

"These include, overall cognitive decline, like dementia, but highly unlikely to have such a profound effect overnight. Drug and alcohol abuse are the more common likelihoods, although I've never known you to experiment with either."

"Is there anything else?"

"Yeah, there's one other possible cause, but although it is the most capable of causing global amnesia, it's the least likely to have occurred."

"Go on."

"You were treated with Electric Convulsive Therapy."

"And you don't think I had ECT?"

"Not likely. It's generally reserved for severe cases of depression, psychosis, mania, and catatonia – none of which I can see you being inflicted with."

Sam raised the palms of his hands skyward. "Hey, people change? Nobody's mental armor is foolproof."

"Agreed. But you're forgetting I spoke to you last night. You weren't exhibiting signs of any of those conditions."

"You can tell over the phone?"

"Yeah," Catarina replied, her voice flat and matter of fact. "The simple fact that you could carry on a well-organized thought process, rules them all out. Besides, the only hospital anywhere nearby that performs ECT is Levanto – so I think we can rule that out."

"So, what's next, Doc?"

"Technically, I'm a professor these days – associate professor that is."

"Really? How old are you?"

She shot him a don't you even dare ask a lady that sort of question glare.

He shrugged. "I'm only saying it, because most people are in their fifties by the time, they secure a professorship… and you don't look anywhere near fifty."

She let him off without a bite. "I'm forty-one."

Sam made a cursory glance at her, trying his best not to be too obvious.

He saw an intelligent, buxom, voluptuous, sexy, completely stunning woman in the prime of her life.

A wry grin creased her lips, as she watched him admire her. "What is it?"

"Nothing." Sam smiled. "You look a hell of a lot better than me, that's all."

She grinned. There was something confident and teasing about it. "I always did."

Sam said, "So what now, professor?"

"Well. I'll be going to sleep soon. I've just finished a night shift. This afternoon, I'll take some bloods from you, and deliver them to the hospital myself. That will tell us what really happened to you in the past twenty-four hours." She met his eye, made a carefully delivered smile that suggested empathy and competence, before squeezing his hand tight. "We'll get to the bottom of this, Sam, I promise."

"Thank you," he replied. "I mean it. I don't know what happened between us, I want to, I really can't remember anything about you or us – but from where I'm sitting, all I can imagine was that I was a real schmuck to ever lose you. You've been a real friend."

"You're welcome. If it makes you feel better, I won't hold it against you, because you can't remember how right you are."

Sam laughed at her joke. Stopped. And then wondered how much of a schmuck he really was.

Catarina caught his pensive mood. "What is it?"

"I need to know what sort of person I am."

"Well. You like to SCUBA dive, you're generally fun to be around, and..." she paused, and smiled lasciviously. "You're not bad in bed – or at least you weren't."

Sam swallowed. One of the greatest regrets in his life right now was that he would never remember it. He shook the thought out of his mind. He had other problems to deal with. "No. I need to know what sort of person I am."

"What do you mean?"

Sam took a breath and said, "I mean, am I a good person, or an asshole."

She laughed. "That one, I can answer."

He held his breath. "Well, which one is it?"

"You're a good person."

"How do you know?"

She met his eye. "Hey, I know."

"But you said you haven't seen me in nearly fifteen years!"

"So?"

Sam persisted. "I might have changed."

"I doubt it. And not by that much. Besides, even if I had never met you, I could tell you that you're a good person."

"Why?"

"Because you're asking the question."

Sam squinted. "What question? What are you talking about?"

"Well. Think about it. An asshole would be asking if he was rich, powerful, feared by people – how good looking his girlfriend was… if he could seduce women and if men admired and feared him."

Sam's lips raised in a slight grin of relief and understanding. "Whereas, I'm asking if I was a good person?"

"Exactly! And, only a good person would care."

Sam grinned. "While we're at it… am I rich?"

She laughed. "As a matter of fact, you are."

"I might not be anymore."

She shook her head. "You couldn't have blown the amount of money your family owned in one lifetime."

"Even if I joined the marines to piss off my dad?" Sam suggested. "Maybe he cut me from my allowance after I failed to make him proud in the family business?"

"I doubt it. It was never like that. The fact was, your father was more disappointed because he expected you to make the company richer. He would have never cut you off if you had something more valuable to do with your time."

"Maybe I became a gambler or got into debt with risky enterprises. Who knows? Just because my dad and grandfather were good at the accumulation of wealth doesn't necessarily mean I would follow suit. Isn't there some sort of statistic that suggests the poor grandparents generally make the money, the children turn it into more money, and the grandchildren blow it all?"

"I don't know. Maybe. But that wasn't you." She grinned. "Besides, unlike most rich people I've met, you always knew you had enough of the stuff. There was never a need to have more. For you, it was just one less thing to have to worry about in life. A means to an end, instead of the other way around."

"That's reassuring to know."

"What do you want to do to kill the time?"

She licked her lips. "I know what we used to do."

He turned his gaze to avoid hers. "I don't know what you're talking about."

"Yes, you do."

"Even so, I don't know if I should be doing that. For all I know, I could be married by now."

"You don't have a ring."

"Maybe I don't wear one. You know, with all the SCUBA diving and stuff?"

"Maybe. But I doubt it. I think I would have heard if you got married."

Sam's eyes darted between her and the couch. She was a beautiful woman. He wanted nothing more than to sleep with her. But he didn't know all the facts. Even though he couldn't recall his history with her, she had told him that he'd broken up with her because he was angry with her, and they hadn't spoken since. Besides, who was to say that he wasn't blissfully married? He didn't wear a wedding ring. But not everyone does.

He shook his head. "I'd better not."

She smiled. "It's just for sleep, nothing more. Like I said, I've just finished a nightshift at the hospital."

Sam didn't need much persuading. "All right."

Chapter Thirteen

National Military Command Center – Pentagon

The NMCC has three main missions, all serving the Chairman of the Joint Chiefs of Staff in his role as the principal military advisor to both the secretary of defense and the president. It was often staffed by dozens of high-ranking military officers, politicians, and civilian experts.

The NMCC is operated by five teams on a rotating watch system. Each team typically has seventeen to twenty personnel on duty performing a wide variety of functions including communications. Teams are led by a Deputy Director for Operations and an Assistant Deputy Director for Operations, and are divided into five duty officer positions.

Today, those numbers were reduced to just three – General Louis C. Painter, the Chairman of the Joint Chiefs of Staff, Margaret Walsh, the Secretary of Defense, and Craig Martin, the Director of the CIA.

The Secretary of Defense looked toward the back, where tired-looking aides and staffers, in civilian clothing, cradled laptops and tablets, talking quietly among themselves. Most of them looked like they hadn't had a chance to change their clothes in the past twenty-four hours.

The Secretary watched the replay of the live aerial footage of the events unfolding at Vernazza, Italy.

She stared at the digital feed coming from the elite team on the ground. Her jaw was set firm, her emerald eyes narrow and piercing. "Captain Borrows, do you mind telling me what the hell went wrong?"

"I'm sorry, Madam Secretary. We were delayed on the road into Vernazza. By the time we reached him, someone else had already attempted to take him out. We tried to intervene, but he ran, and we haven't been able to make contact since. And then…"

"He jumped into the ocean."

"That's right, ma'am. The Italian Polizia have been searching for him with a police search and rescue helicopter – I'm afraid he might be dead. I'm very sorry."

The Secretary's mouth was set hard. "If Sam Reilly jumped into the sea, I'm willing to bet everything we have, he's still alive – so you'd better hope to hell you find him before the Polizia do!"

Captain Borrows said, "Yes, ma'am."

Chapter Fourteen

Andre stepped on board the ghost ship.

The rusty steel decking creaked under his footsteps, and for a moment he wondered whether the archaic fishing boat would take his weight. His eyes swept the ship's topside with curiosity.

If he had to guess, and he was by no means a sailor or in any position to make an educated assessment of such things, he imagined the ship had been drifting at sea for some years, before randomly washing up into the medieval harbor of Vernazza.

The police chief caught his attention. "There's a hatch over here. You can go inside if you like. It doesn't look like much. There are no signs of anyone living on board recently. I'm starting to wonder if your red card was even connected to the ghost ship at all."

Andre made a wry smile. "It's a possibility. I mean, it's not like Sam Reilly used this boat to sail here. Of course, that still leaves the question of how he got here in the first place."

"Maybe someone dropped him off from a mother ship, and he just rowed into the harbor."

"Sure. But if you're going to do that, why bring the girl you just murdered? Why not dispose of her body in the sea for God's sake? He must have known her body would immediately bring with it a crime investigation?"

The police chief held the hatchway open for him. "No idea. If you happen to work that one out, you let me know, won't you?"

"Of course."

Andre ducked down, and climbed into the decks below.

The inside of the ship seemed barren, but otherwise in much better shape than she was above decks. It made him wonder whether the hatch had been closed all these years, protecting the inside of the hull, while time and seawater corrosion decimated the outside of the ship.

He shined a small flashlight around the hull.

Careful not to let the hatchway close and somehow trap him inside, he headed deeper into the ship. The place was dry. The air, stale and musky. He walked around for a little while, before stopping to carefully pace out the full length of the internal hull. He reached the end and stopped.

Glancing up at the police chief, he asked, "Where's the rest of the boat?"

"What rest of it?" the police chief replied, his palms facing upward. "What you see is what you get."

"No, it isn't," Andre said, emphatically. "I've never been a sailor and I can't say I know much about boats, but I do know that this isn't the entire boat."

The police chief shot a puzzled look at him. "It isn't?"

"No. For one thing, where's the cockpit? Boats, even ghost ships, need a helm or somewhere to steer the boat from. Then there's the issue of an engine room, sleeping quarters, toilets… there's nothing in here."

"Maybe the place has been stripped by salvagers?"

"No. There's more to it than that. If someone went to the trouble to gut this ship, they would have extracted the steel from her hull. Mark my words, there would be more here than we're looking at. Find its second hull, and we'll find answers to our mystery."

"You're that confident?"

"Yes! The length of the exterior hull, taken from my assessment on the deck is precisely seventy-nine feet in length, yet the internal hull is just sixty. So, you want to take a guess where those other nineteen feet disappeared to? Also, we've lost nearly four feet on either side of her beam. You know what this means, right?"

The police chief's eyes narrowed. "There's a double hull."

Andre said, "Exactly! And I think I know why."

The police chief glanced at him. A mental image of the ship out of water appeared to be coming to him, giving credence to the theory. He turned to one of his officers. "Go back to the shore. I want two UV light sticks. If there's a secret door, I want it found."

"Understood, sir."

A few minutes later, the police chief reappeared with a pair of UV lights. It was amazing what things the UV light highlighted. The iron from removed blood, sweat, salt, and other human byproducts ordinarily hidden from the naked eye, became radiant under the UV rays. He handed one to Andre and kept the other one to use himself.

Andre took the UV light, switched it on, and then switched off his own flashlight, leaving them in the dark blue haze. He slowly walked the length of the ship's hull, searching for signs of human presence. There was very little evidence of human habitation. If anything, he was starting to return to his original theory that the ghost ship had nothing to do with Sam Reilly.

Maybe it really was just one hell of a coincidence the ghost ship washed up into the harbor of Vernazza the same night Sam Reilly happened to make an attempt to survive. It didn't really matter to him. In the end, all he wanted to do was make certain that the man hadn't left anything incriminating on board – anything that might bring down his employer.

He'd been paid to complete a kill contract, but as a loyal servant, he would be remiss if he were to leave evidence, allowing the truth – which Sam Reilly was in possession of – to come out anyway. No. He needed to be certain.

He turned and headed toward the stern.

About eight feet from the edge, he stopped and grinned. There was a small outline that looked like a series of handprints.

But no door handle, no latch, and no sign of anywhere to go.

Andre frowned.

Behind him, the chief of the police asked, "Find anything?"

"I don't know. This whole area here lights up with evidence of hundreds of hand prints, carefully placed on exactly this same location."

The chief stared at it. "The door, if there is a door, is perfectly sealed. Someone has gone to great lengths to keep its location hidden."

"Mark my words, there's a door right there."

As if to prove the point, the door flung open.

A figure in dark clothing and wearing a black balaclava, stepped out, grabbed the chief of police, and dragged him inside again – like a predator in the night.

Leaving Andre all alone and unable to enter the locked door.

Chapter Fifteen

Andre tried to blink the foggy haze out of his mind.

The door had smacked him in the face as it opened with such force that it nearly rendered him unconscious.

He kicked at the door, but it didn't budge. His heart was pounding. He had it. He's close. He just needed to get inside that damned door.

He withdrew a silenced, Heckler and Koch, Mark 23 semi-automatic pistol. He leveled the weapon at the section of the near-invisible hatchway where the handprints were confined, and paused, contemplating shooting at it. He dismissed the thought in an instant. The internal hull was made of steel – his .45 ACP rounds would barely dent it, before most likely ricocheting and killing him in the process.

He gave the door one solid kick with his boot.

Andre gave a loud grunt.

It certainly felt like kicking steel. The intricate web of tendons and ligaments that held the patella –that small flat bone that acts as a protective cover for the knee joints – felt like it was going to snap.

His jaw hardened, and the lines around his face deepened. He was reacting on instinct and reflexes. Not the way he usually operated. His best-case scenario – what he really wanted and needed to do – was get through that hatch, kill everyone inside, and close the hatch again.

But that was no longer an option.

He needed help.

If he could get some reinforcements and a welder, there might just possibly still be time to go in, and kill everyone. Maybe, if he acted fast enough, and told the polizia about someone taking their chief captive, he might still have a chance to succeed. It would mean more collateral damage. For a start, the chief of police couldn't be allowed to survive, given what he must already now know. And next, everyone who came on board to help him would need to die.

He didn't like it.

It would be a lot of collateral deaths.

Not that he was squeamish about that – after all, he was first and foremost, a paid hitman... maybe with a better ID badge, and the pretense of a perfectly respectable job with Interpol, but none of that removed the simple fact that he was paid money in exchange for murdering people he knew nothing about.

The issue here, was that amount of collateral damage meant that there were bound to be consequences.

And for a man in his trade, that was unforgivable.

He frowned.

Still, he was out of options.

Andre climbed the stairs, through the hatch, and onto the deck.

He spotted a crew of detectives heading his way on an inflatable Zodiac at full speed. He waved his arms to them.

"Quick!" he shouted. "I need help!"

The person at the Zodiac's controls steered straight for him.

Andre glanced at the clear water beneath the stern. He could see the sandy seabed thirty feet below as though he could touch it. There was a small ripple of movement. Nothing much, but whatever it was, it caught his eye.

He leaned over the gnarled web of rusty metal to get a better look.

And an instant later, the rusty deck began to vibrate. The deep gurgling sound of a high-powered engine came to life. The ripple of water behind the stern turned into a powerful twin waterjet.

Andre tried to grip something for balance, but the entire topside of the decrepit ghost ship was liquid rust, making it slippery.

As the ghost ship lurched forward, he slipped onto his back with a loud and painful thump.

The ship's bow lifted up, and he rolled off the back of the stern, landing in the warm water below. He kicked hard to reach the surface. It was always harder to swim in boots. His head surfaced and he took a deep breath.

He squinted, but already, the fast-moving ghost ship was on the aquaplane, skimming the water at speeds in excess of seventy knots, and disappearing far beyond the breakwater, into the Tyrrhenian Sea.

Chapter Sixteen

Fifty-Six Hours

Sam Reilly woke up feeling content.

He opened his eyes. Catarina was there next to him. She wore a singlet without a bra, revealing her soft, voluptuous body, and the slight hint of her nipples. Her exotic face was set with a mischievous grin, and her beguiling gray eyes teased him, as she ran her fingers through his hair.

"Good morning," he said, pleased to know he could still remember her. That meant his memory wasn't completely damaged. It wasn't like dementia which permanently altered the brain's ability to catalogue memories.

"Good afternoon," she replied.

"How long did I sleep?"

"About three hours."

"That's all?"

"Afraid so. We have things to do. How do you feel?"

"Good. I think."

"What about your memory?"

"I remember meeting you this morning."

She grinned. "I'm hard to forget."

He nodded, pleasure and desire plastered on his face. "Yes, you most certainly are. I still can't believe I can't remember you from before."

She smiled, her eyes fixed on him, with a curious and puzzling look, as her eyes traced his naked chest, her fingers running over his muscular physique, and array of scars.

Sam asked, "What?"

"Nothing."

"Seriously? What is it? Have I changed that much since…?"

"It has been at least fifteen years."

"And?"

"You look exactly the same…"

"Except?"

"There's a few more battle wounds. Jesus, it looks like you've been shot here on your shoulder, once or twice in your chest, and once in your abdomen." Her hand moved delicately across his lower torso. "And what is this? A stab wound?"

Sam shrugged. "I wouldn't know. My body is as new to me as it is to you."

"You look like you haven't treated it very well since I last saw you naked," she chided, her voice set like a doctor disciplining a patient for smoking.

"Hey, it's not like I can remember my mistakes!"

She stood up slowly out of the bed. She had a pair of black Italian knickers that covered her dark tanned skin. She was neither fat nor skinny. Her figure was perfectly proportioned.

Even after only three hours sleep, she was sexy.

Catarina caught him looking at her. She smiled. "And me… have I changed?"

He held her gaze. "I have no idea. Were you entirely perfect last time we met?"

"Yes."

He laughed. "Then, I'd say you haven't changed a bit."

"Good. I'm glad to hear that." Her lips parted in a lascivious smile. "Last night was nice by the way. It was exactly as I remember it."

"I wish I could remember it. But all the same, I'm happy to make new memories."

She held his gaze. "I'd like that to be true."

"It is," he said, his voice firm. "I just wish I could remember why I was angry with you all those years ago."

She played with his thick brown hair, met his eyes, and kissed him. "Does it matter?"

Sam shrugged. "It might. Right now, I can't imagine what you could have possibly done to make me so angry that I was willing to leave you." He studied her response, hoping to see something in it. "I don't suppose you want to tell me what it was, before I get in too deep?"

"No. I'm afraid I've been given a second chance, and I don't want to wreck it – not yet anyway."

He tried to argue, but instead, she kissed him again.

She stood up. "Get dressed. I'll take some blood from you and get it checked out at the hospital right away. Then, on my way back, I'll try and pick up your suitcase."

"Thanks."

Ten minutes later, they were both dressed. She put a tourniquet on his left arm, found a vein, inserted a needle, and withdrew a blood sample into a vacu-container.

She glanced at his arms. There was a small red dot in the inside crease of his elbow. She frowned.

Sam asked, "What?"

"It looks like you've recently had a blood test in this arm."

"Really?"

"Yeah, see… right here. Someone's performed venipuncture, either to take a sample of blood, or put something in."

Sam said, "Like a drug addict, injecting something?"

"Exactly."

"So you think I might have become a drug addict?"

"No, I doubt it. Like I said before, you don't have that sort of personality."

"So then why do I have track marks?"

"Track marks refer to a line of injection sites, commonly found on intravenous drug user's arms, where they have injected continuously. This is just one injection site."

"All right. So what does it mean?"

"I don't know. Maybe you just injected once? Or maybe you had an operation and someone gave you antibiotics afterward? I don't know. We'll find out as soon as I get this sample to the lab."

She sealed the blood sample in a snap-lock pathology collection bag, with the ring contained within three rings, the international symbol for a biohazard.

"I'll take this to the pathology labs at the hospital," she said. "I'll do the test myself. It won't take long. I should be back in a couple hours. I'll try my best to have some answers for you. If *Via Visconti* is empty, I'll retrieve that suitcase for you, too."

Sam stopped her from leaving. "Catarina…"

"Yes?"

"Thank you. For everything. I mean it. You've been a life saver."

"You're welcome," she said.

Catarina stepped up to meet him, wrapped her arms around his neck. Her lips parted, and she kissed his mouth. It was a slow caress, tender, yet passionate. She was painfully sexy. In her own Italian way, she made the simple act of kissing seem to have all the passion and pleasure of making love.

A moment later, she pulled back, opened the door – and disappeared from sight.

Chapter Seventeen

Tom Bower kept his eyes fixed on the graphical display screen in front of him.

It utilized the same heads-up display technology used by pilots on fighter jets, only in this case, it was projecting a live feed from high definition video cameras mounted at the front of the ghost ship. His right hand gripped a joystick. He was concentrating hard, making tiny adjustments, threading the ship through a small flotilla of sailing yachts at their anchorage.

He'd broken past the coast guard search and rescue vessel, but two jet skis had given chase. He was in the process of dragging them through the rougher waters near the coastline in an attempt to force them to slow down or get knocked off.

Tom glanced at the GPS display map. They were heading south along the Italian coast, moving at nearly fifty knots, swerving in and out of an array of jagged coastal rocks.

He made a quick shift with his hand, darted between a narrow tidal constriction, between a series of thirty-foot-high sea stacks and the point at the edge of the Riomaggiore harbor.

His bow wave ripped against the rocks, sending a tidal-wave-like response as it ebbed. The two jet skis responded badly. One tried to ride the wave, but pulled back too hard, and ended landing on his back in the water, while the other one attempted to make a sudden ninety degree turn, abandon the chase, and backtrack around the sea stacks.

Tom came out the opposite side and into the open sea.

He increased the throttle to full. Released from its earthly restraints, the ghost ship picked up speed, racing ahead at nearly seventy-five knots.

Tom glanced at the rear-view camera display.

One down and one lagging too far behind to catch him now that he was in the open water.

Then he swore, because the police rescue helicopter had joined the pursuit.

He kept the ghost ship on a southerly route.

Using his left hand, he expanded the GPS display using a reverse pinch grip, until the map showed the next fifty miles of coastal regions.

His eyes scanned the area, searching for somewhere to take refuge from the now permanent set of eyes, tracking them like a bird of prey, on board the police helicopter.

He considered the French Island of Corsica. An Italian police helicopter chasing an unidentified boat might at the very least prove a diplomatic problem for them, but was unlikely to last long enough to aid him at all. Besides, the island was roughly fifty miles away, across open ocean. It would be too easy for the pilot to notify the French coast guard and possibly get their assistance.

No, he needed somewhere closer.

He turned his attention to the Tuscan Archipelago, a series of seven islands that followed the coast of Italy belonging to the Province of Livorno. Capraia was the closest, but Elba and Giglio were bigger, allowing more likelihood of a sea cave, or grotto in which he might take refuge.

But he dismissed them as being too far out to be feasible. It still meant traveling along the open ocean. Even if it worked on the outward journey, it would never work for the return trip. No. They needed to stay along the Italian Riviera.

What he needed was something nearby. Something he could use to hide just long enough to make the transformation.

His eyes locked onto Grotta dell'Arpaia, on the coast of *Port Venere.*

Tom clicked the location, bringing up information about the region.

The coastal town of Port Venere was famous for its sea caves. Grotta dell'Arpaia, being its largest and most famous, was named after Lord George Byron, a poet who swam out to it to meet a girl in secret, and said to be the inspiration of much of his poetry work. Unfortunately, the large grotto had long since collapsed.

Nearby, the region included several sea caves, including Azzurra and Blue Cave, Tinetto – the cavity of the Doves and the wall of Tino, the shoal of Dante and Small and Big Creeks.

He zoomed in.

Azzurra was massive, and during the day often had several tourist boats.

It was perfect.

Tom steered a direct course for the sea cave.

Behind him, and still dressed in a black skivvy, Genevieve came up. She was lithe, and muscular. She had short brown hair, blue eyes, and a grin that told him they were in trouble. She'd joined Sam Reilly's team several years ago now, as somewhat of a mystery. A woman of mixed talents, she could cook and kill in equally admirable proportions. Since then, they had discovered that she had once been an assassin working for her father, who headed the Russian mafia. A deadly history, which Tom had tried to forget in the past three years the two of them had been dating.

She was followed by a man in a police uniform.

"Tom, we have a problem back here."

Tom glanced at her, his eyes focused on the task at hand, navigating around an upcoming fleet of small fishing boats. His eyes darted toward the police helicopter hovering above. "We have a problem up here, too. What's wrong?"

"It appears I grabbed the wrong man…"

"What?"

"This is Mr. Gabriele Valentino, the Chief of Police for La Spezia."

Tom met the man's hardened stare. "Tom Bower. My apologies, sir. We can explain everything, but right now, we're in a bit of a pickle. So, I'm afraid, you're just going to have to sit tight."

The police chief arced up. "Wait just a minute..."

"I understand you're rightfully pissed off. Unfortunately, you've just interrupted an international project that's been in the pipeline for nearly a year."

"No, I don't think you understand me..." the police chief tried to stand up, his gesture threatening, and his voice hard.

Genevieve gave his wrist a subtle twist, and he gave a sharp welp.

Tom said, "Be nice, Genevieve. It's not this man's fault that you interrupted his investigation by accidentally taking the wrong man." He turned to meet the chief's eye. "Sorry, sir. What were you saying?"

The police chief raised his voice, glanced at Genevieve, and then carefully lowered it again. "I was saying, I'm the chief of police for La Spezia, my brother is the mayor, and my uncle is a senator..."

Tom interrupted him. "And this project was signed off by your president, so I'm afraid you're just going to have to be a little patient a while longer."

The chief caught his eye. "You're lying."

"Hey, we're the good guys..."

"I don't believe you! You're lying."

"I'm not. I'll be happy to show you some written documents to prove it shortly. But, as you can tell, we're in a bit of trouble. If you'd like, you're welcome to take a seat and watch the show... or, I can leave you in the back, under Genevieve's guard."

The police chief glanced at her, his eyes darting back to Tom. "Ah, no thank you. I think I'll wait here with you."

"Very good."

Ten minutes later, Tom slowed the engine and the ghost ship dropped off the aquaplane and pulled into the protective cover of the *Azzurra* sea cave.

Overhead, the police helicopter hovered, taking up a waiting position.

Inside the cave were three other tourist ships.

Tom brought the ship to a complete stop. He opened a digital control panel and switched off a series of locking mechanisms.

The police chief asked, "What is this?"

Tom grinned. "A little bit of subterfuge."

He pressed the release button and immediately the hydraulic arms lifted the entire, rusty top deck off the ghost ship. It was nothing more than a façade of rust, draped over a frame of particle board. The canopy dropped overboard, sinking to the seabed below.

The police chief met his eye, accusingly.

Tom said, "What? I promise we'll be back to pick that up in a few days."

When the process was complete, Tom pressed a second lever, labeled, *ballast.*

The ballast gates opened, and the ghost ship's hull filled with water. The weight dragged the ship's hull deeper into the water.

Tom grinned. "All right, let's go."

The chief asked, "Where?"

"Back to Vernazza, of course. There's work to be done…"

Chapter Eighteen

Inside the cockpit of the police helicopter, the pilot reported that a small, modern fishing boat left the *Azzurra* sea cave.

Standing at the helm was a tall guy, most likely a tourist, out for a day on the water.

The pilot took note of the vessel, but dismissed it as being irrelevant, because it was merely a quarter of the size of the ghost ship.

And had an open wheel house, with no canopy or covered section below its decks.

Chapter Nineteen

Sam Reilly watched Catarina enter the apartment again.

Her face was even more striking than he remembered, but it was set with worry.

"What is it?" he asked. "Did you have any luck?"

"I did. I got the blood tests and the suitcase," she said, handing him the metallic case.

He took it and glanced at the case, wanting to open it right away, but decided to wait. He needed to know what she had found.

When she didn't say anything, he asked, "What is it? What did you find?"

"Your blood results came back with a combination of benzodiazepines, barbiturates, and opioids."

Sam looked up. "Great. Does any of that explain my amnesia?"

"I think so."

"So, does that mean, when they wear off, I'll start to remember things?"

"It might, but probably not as fast as you're hoping." She sat down next to him and took his hand. Her face was full of concern and otherwise unreadable. Her eyes darting away, trying to avoid his gaze, as though she was undecided about how much to say or in what order to say it.

"There's something else?" he asked.

"Yeah."

"All right. So tell me."

"Do you know anything about Electric Convulsive Therapy?"

Sam's lips parted in a smile. "No. I can't say I do."

"It's predominantly used as a last line of treatment options in patients suffering from severe depression, mania, psychosis, and catatonia by altering the blood chemistry in the person's brain."

"Okay, if you say so," Sam said, waiting to see where this would go.

"That exact cocktail of drugs found in your system is commonly used during ECT." She waited for his reaction to the news. Finding none, she continued. "The barbiturates are used as an anaesthetic sedative to make you unconscious and unaware of the procedure, whereas, the benzodiazepines are muscles relaxants designed to help minimize the seizure and prevent injury, and the opioid, blurs your perception of any residual pain."

"You think I had ECT?"

She nodded. "I'm pretty certain you did."

"So I'm crazy?" He felt a lump in his throat that made him want to choke. His face was crestfallen. "Is that it? I've escaped an insane asylum and gone on a killing spree?"

"I don't think it's like that at all."

"It sure seems like the most plausible option. Maybe I should call the police now, before I have the chance to kill anyone else?"

"It's okay, I don't think you're suffering with a mental illness or that you've just escaped from an insane asylum."

"Then what?"

She paused. Took her time and made her words deliberate. "The most common side effects of ECT are confusion and memory loss. Immediately after treatment, you may experience confusion, which can last from a few minutes to several hours. You may not know where you are or why you're there. Rarely, confusion may last several days or longer."

"But it comes back?"

"Some of it, but not all. Some people have trouble remembering events that occurred right before treatment or in the weeks or months before treatment or, rarely, from previous years. This condition is called retrograde amnesia, or in your case, global amnesia. You may also have trouble recalling events that occurred during the weeks of your treatment. For most people, these memory problems usually improve within a couple of months after treatment ends."

"Well, that rules out any chance of me getting my memory back before I need to be at The Hague in the next couple days."

"Probably."

She looked worried.

Sam said, "What aren't you telling me?"

"You're right. I'm keeping something from you and you have a right to know. Worse than that, you need to know."

"Go on."

"The hospital I work at in *Levanto* performs ECT. I checked the register. There was one male person who had ECT performed last night. The register said his name was *Pinco Pallino* and under diagnosis, was simply the words, *ongoing treatment*, and the medical authority for the procedure was by a Dr. *Tal dei Tali.*"

"Okay… so what does that mean?"

Catarina looked sympathetic. "First off, *Pinco Pallino*, is the Italian equivalent of *John Doe*, used in the place of a patient's name when their details aren't yet known. But ECT is used as a last line of treatment options, in patients with long term mental health problems, untreatable using traditional drug therapy and counseling."

"Any chance maybe the guy's name really was *Pinco Pallino?*"

"It's possible. But pretty unlikely."

"But not impossible?" Sam asked, hopeful. "So, can't you ask the authorizing doctor?"

"Ordinarily I could, but the doctor in charge of the procedure was from out of area."

"Does that happen very often?"

"It's not uncommon. Psychiatrists rotate in and out of the region. Sometimes, patients who have unusually complex histories, might be transferred here from out of area, for specific treatment. Psychiatrists get sick and sometimes we bring in locums from outside… so it's not impossible."

"Okay, so what did the doctor say?"

"Nothing. I couldn't track her down."

"Why not?"

"Because *Tal dei Tali* is the Italian equivalent of *Jane Doe*. But the most compelling evidence was the anesthesiologist records."

"Why? What did they say?"

"They didn't leave any more details about who you were or where you had come from, but they did identify you as six foot exactly and a hundred and seventy-five pounds."

Sam glanced at himself in the reflection of the window. "How close am I to that?"

"We could weigh you if I had any scales – which I don't – but I didn't need to."

Sam swallowed hard. "What are you saying?"

Catarina squeezed his hand sympathetically, and met his eye. "I'm saying… this didn't happen to you by chance… someone intentionally did this to you."

Chapter Twenty

Sam let that thought sink in.

Someone had intentionally erased his memory. That much was now a certainty. They had gone to the trouble of drugging and sedating him so that they could perform ECT on him for the sole purpose of taking away his memory.

The question was, why?

What did he know that was so valuable that someone would want to go to such extreme lengths to make him forget?

For that matter, why not kill him in the first place? None of it made any sense.

Catarina asked, "Are you okay?"

Sam grinned. "Sure. Why not? I've lost my memory as the direct result of someone taking it from me, but it turns out that I've got a great life, and I've managed to rekindle a relationship with a beautiful woman, what's not to like?"

Her lips parted in a restrained smile. She'd been a doctor long enough to know when someone was protecting themselves under the mental armor of a happy disposition and a façade of positivity. "It's going to be all right. Your memory, most of it, will come back."

"I wonder if you will still be here when it does."

She took his hand and kissed it. "I will be if you want me to."

Sam looked at her. "Thank you."

They waited in silence for another couple seconds. He tried to process the news as best he could. Failing to come up with any answer, he returned to the data he'd neglected that was still in front of him.

A slight grin creased his lips. "What about the suitcase?"

"You're right. Open the suitcase... maybe it will clear you of all wrongdoing, and make sense of everything... or at least something."

"Or maybe it will prove that I'm part of the Russian mafia?"

"I doubt it."

Sam said, "I'm not sure I am yet..."

"I am," she replied, a tease of laugher in her voice. "But I can't rule out the Italian mafia..."

He laughed out loud, a sudden tension easing in the process.

For some reason he hadn't even considered that as a possibility, but it certainly made more sense, after all, he was in Italy. If the Russian mafia had a problem with him, he would have been more likely to have woken up in Moscow.

"All right," he said, "let's open it."

She put the suitcase on the coffee table.

Sam grabbed it and pulled it toward him. It was a metallic case that looked unnaturally military or clandestine – something one would expect to be seen carrying the nuclear codes for the president. The sight of it reassured him that he'd made the right decision by stashing it when he had, instead of trying to carry it with him. He would have stood out too much, and would almost definitely have been arrested by now otherwise.

He flipped the suitcase over.

It was made from some sort of metallic alloy, and designed so that each side slid in perfectly together, barely revealing any opening at all. There were no obvious locking mechanisms. Nothing external that could be broken off.

There was a piece of protective metal, a small sliver no longer than a person's thumb, which covered something.

Unable to see anything else to work with, Sam slid it open.

Inside was a digital touch screen with eight numbers.

Sam frowned.

Catarina asked, "What have you got?"

"It needs me to enter an eight-digit numerical code."

She made a pensive pause. "Eight digits… like a date of birth?"

"Sure. But whose?"

"I would try yours first."

"That seems a little obvious. I mean, if I was, presumably, carrying something vitally important, don't you think I would have used a better security code than my date of birth?"

"Sure. Unless, you specifically wanted to find it?"

"Why would I do that?"

"I don't know. What if you knew someone was trying to erase your memory? Maybe you left yourself some sort of clue to get it back again?"

"Does the brain work like that?" Sam asked, his voice hopeful. "I mean, is it likely an image, sound, taste, or smell will trigger a memory, and like a cascade, my whole life will come back?"

"Not really, but definitely little things will help. If you have been treated with electric convulsive therapy, depending on the number of courses you have been bombarded with, the global amnesia can last anywhere between a matter of hours, through to days and weeks, but eventually you should regain some if not most of your long-term memories."

"Why?"

"Who knows? The human brain's an amazing computer. No one really understands how it works."

"I thought you were meant to be a leading expert on memory loss?"

"I am." She smiled. "Why do you think I'm studying the human brain and trying to map out how it categorizes data – AKA memories?"

Sam asked, "So what happens in my case?"

"In global amnesia, you mean?"

"Yeah."

Catarina answered without hesitation, like a lecturer, who'd given a speech on the subject more than a dozen times. "In its simplest form, the human brain, attempts to store memories in giant databases, categorizing specific memories by date, time, and relevant event. In fact, over the course of your lifetime, your brain will store every single sense – we're talking sight, sound, smell, touch, and taste here – and it will store them forever."

"Wait… you're telling me the human brain stores everything we've ever done."

"Yep."

"Then, why do people need to study for anything? I mean, if the brain's already storing it, why do we need to keep studying material over and over again until it becomes stored in our memory? I'm sure I would have done better at college if I retained everything the first-time round."

"Ah, good question." Her eyes sparkled with delight. "It has to do with categorizing the database. You see, the human brain likes to associate things together, cataloguing them by sight – for example, a cat and by any other senses, received, such as the feeling of patting a soft furry creature, and smell of flea powder."

"Okay…" Sam said, waiting for the problem.

"The problem comes with the simple fact that you might have hundreds if not thousands of images of cats in your database – hey, I'm not judging you here – but the reality is, the human brain knows that you have no need for all of them, so it subconsciously tries to attach more relevance to the most important images. For example, if you received a cat on your fifth birthday, assuming it was a good one, your brain would have been fed with a number of neurochemicals, such as dopamine, oxytocin, serotonin, and endorphins making you feel happy. Alternatively, if you were attacked by a cat, your brain would have been fed increased levels of adrenaline and nor-adrenaline, which your brain then registers that event as important, in case it needs to be suddenly cross-referenced at a later date – you know, if you see a cat again, you shouldn't get too close or it will scratch at you."

"So the problem is in that cataloguing of information, not the recording?"

"Exactly."

"Right. Let's hope whatever's inside here happens to be the key."

"So open it."

"I still don't have a clue about the password."

"Try your birthday."

"I don't even know my own birthday!"

"See!" she said. "Exactly. What a perfect password for a man who's lost his memory?"

"I don't suppose you remember it, do you?"

She grinned. "Of course I do."

She read out his date of birth. He committed it to memory, hoping that his brain would take the appropriate measure to categorize it correctly so that he could find it again later. Somehow, one's own birthdate seemed like something pretty important to know.

He typed the eight-digit number into the keypad and pressed enter.

The numbers flashed, and the case remained locked.

Sam said, "I told you it wouldn't work."

Catarina bit her lower lip, her face expressive, and inquisitive. "What if you changed the numbers around?"

"In what way?"

"Put the days of the month in first, followed by the month, then the year."

"Why?"

"Because your mother was Australian, and like the rest of the world, that's the way they write dates."

"You think it's another trick within a trick? Once my memory developed enough that I could remember my date of birth, I still needed to remember that my mother was Australian? It seems pretty far-fetched."

She grinned. "Hey, there's nothing about your story that is anything but far-fetched."

Sam laughed. "All right."

He input the eight-digit number, using the Australian date formatting.

A moment later, the numbers flashed, as they had previously.

Sam said, "See... I told you it wouldn't work."

Then it clicked open.

She caught his glance. "You were saying?"

Sam swallowed. "Moment of truth. Who am I? A good person having a bad day, or a bad person getting his comeuppance?"

"You're not involved in organized crime and you're not with the Russian mafia!"

"If you say so."

He opened the suitcase.

Inside were several piles of US hundred-dollar notes. At a glance, each bundle had a hundred notes or ten thousand dollars. There were ten bundles, meaning there was a hundred thousand US dollars in cash. Next to it was a similar pile of Russian 5,000-ruble notes. He did the math, and instinctively knew the rough exchange rate. There was 6.5 million rubles. The equivalent of a hundred thousand US dollars.

Separating the two different currencies, were a series of six passports.

Sam picked up one of them, opened it. The face was his own. The name, date of birth, and country, all foreign.

He picked up the rest of the passports, and ran his fingers through them.

They were all his passports.

All perfectly produced fakes.

There was only one more item among the treasure filled suitcase. An old video cassette with no name on it.

Sam took a deep breath and crossed his arms. "Still don't believe I'm involved with the Russian Mafia?"

Chapter Twenty-One

Sam watched Catarina's reaction.

Her gaze darted from the suitcase back to him. "All right, I admit, it looks pretty bad."

Sam showed her the fake passports. "Hey, the good news is, if I'm not involved in organized crime, chances are I'm a spy... the downside of course, I really don't know what I'm fighting for or on whose side I am."

Catarina picked up the video cassette. "Maybe this might tell you?"

"Yeah, maybe. Who the hell uses a VHS anymore?"

She frowned. "Nobody. Whoever put information on this wanted to make it difficult for anyone to find."

Sam shrugged. "Sure. It's going to be difficult, but not impossible. I'm sure a quick search on eBay would reveal several of the antique VCRs for next to nothing."

"Yeah, but that's going to take time. Whoever left you with that suitcase probably knew that if you broke the code and got inside, you'd struggle to find a VCR in time to play it before the seventy-two hours were up and you were supposed to be in The Hague."

"So, we just need to get really lucky and find some old timer nearby who still likes to watch old movies on VHS?"

She stared at the tape and frowned. "It gets worse than that."

"Really? How?"

"This isn't VHS, it's a Betamax."

Chapter Twenty-Two

Sam sighed. "What's a Betamax? Is Betamax some sort of new invention that I can't remember? Something to do with the whole global amnesia thing?"

"No. It's older than VHS. Betamax was first released in 1975 while VHS trailed along with its release in 1976. What ensued was a bitter format war, which ultimately was won by VHS."

Sam's eyes narrowed. "How do you know this stuff?"

She shrugged. "I remember my dad mentioning it somewhere. What can I say, I retain useless information? It's one of the oddities of the human brain and its unique cataloguing system. I can tell you exact dates of random facts, but had to take my biochemistry exams twice."

"Okay, so now I need to find someone really old. What sort of movies were originally played on Betamax? Maybe an aficionado of some classic films might still have a Betamax player?"

She blushed and bit her lower lip. "You sure you want to know?"

He grinned. "Don't keep me waiting. We're only talking about my life here…"

Her eyes flashed. "It was used to bring adult films into the private homes of viewers…"

Sam paused, taking that in for a moment. He said, "You mean… we now have to find a porn dealer who specializes in classic originals from 1975?"

She shrugged. "Like I said, whoever placed this recording here, did so knowing full well that it would take you weeks to find out what was recorded on it."

Sam shoved the tape in the suitcase and closed it.

Sam said, "I don't suppose you know of any nearby antique stores?"

"Nothing that's likely to stock a Betamax."

"There must be a better way of doing this. What about my friends?"

"What about them?"

"Surely I must have friends, right? You said I wasn't an asshole, so where are all my friends... you know, the ones who will drop whatever it is they're doing and come help you out when the proverbial fecal matter hits the fan?"

"Good question. I don't know. It's been a long time. Like I said, with the exception of last night, I haven't spoken to you in a very long time."

"But what about my friends when we were together. You said we were together for two years. Surely I must have introduced you to some of my friends in that time?"

She grimaced. "To be honest, we traveled a lot. Did a lot of things on our own."

"Really. I'm starting to think maybe my life wasn't so rosy. Surely, I had other friends?"

She paused and thought about it. "Wait... you had a best friend. A big guy... you played sports, and SCUBA dived and competed in everything together. I think you were even talking about joining the marines together?"

A best friend. That sounds better. "What's his name?"

"Tom Bower."

"Any chance you still have his cell number?"

She laughed. "When we were together, I didn't even own a cell phone."

"Really?"

"No. We had cell phones. But I never got Tom's number. Don't worry, I have the internet. I'm sure I can find out."

"Great."

A few minutes of Googling later and she found what they needed. "It says here that you're working for your dad's company in shipping."

"Really? Sounds boring. So my dad won out after all and I joined the family business?"

"It would appear so." Catarina continued to scroll down the webpage. "Apparently you head up a salvage and rescue vessel, named the *Tahila*."

"Nice name," Sam said. "I wonder what it means?"

"Who knows. Probably something your dad liked?"

"Probably. What does she look like?"

Catarina clicked on the link and the image of the ship came up. "Woah! That doesn't look like a salvage vessel. That looks more like a cross between a luxury yacht and a battleship."

Sam grinned. "Maybe my job's less boring than it first sounded?"

Leaning over her shoulder, he clicked on the link titled, *Expeditions and Discoveries.*

The webpage opened up and a long list of accolades unfolded.

Sam ran his eyes across them...

Located the Mahogany Ship

Discovered remnants of the Stolen City of Atlantis

Located the Last Airship, named Magdalena

Traversed the Aleutian Portal...

Sam said, "These read like bad adventure novels..."

"Hey, you've been busy..."

"Looks like it. Wish I could remember some of it."

"Maybe you will one day?"

"I hope so. Hey, click on crew members."

It brought up a list of people who worked in his team. None of them familiar to him.

Sam asked, "Which one's Tom Bower?"

"The one on the left."

There was a guy a good head taller than the rest and probably another fifty pounds heavier, built out of solid muscle, too. "The big guy?"

"That's him. Hasn't changed a bit. Aged better than you..."

Sam ignored the tease. "Can you see any contact details?"

"There's his cell phone."

Sam looked at the number, committed it to his memory, and asked, "Mind if I borrow your phone?"

Chapter Twenty-Three

Sam dialed the number.

"Hello?" The voice was hesitant… like someone receiving an unrecognized call, and not yet sure they wanted to commit to talking to the person on the other side.

Sam said, "Tom Bower?"

There was relief in the man's voice. "Good God, Sam! You're alive!"

Chapter Twenty-Four

Sam hung up the phone.

They had talked for less than two minutes. But the conversation was easy and came naturally. It was clear the two of them had an affinity for each other that came with a friendship that had developed over many years.

Catarina asked, "Any luck?"

"Yeah. He says I was on a secret mission two nights ago. He was supposed to pick me up at the beach here in Vernazza, but I never made it back."

"Did he say what the mission was for?"

"No. He said he didn't want to get into any of the details over the phone, because he couldn't be certain the line was secure."

"What the hell does that even mean?" Catarina asked. "Maybe you are a spy? I mean, why else all the cloak and dagger stuff? The array of fake passports? Tom Bower's been your best friend since you were a kid and he couldn't recognize your voice well enough to be confident that he was speaking to you, and able to fill you in with what you were doing when you had your memory stolen from you?"

Sam twisted his hands outward, in a gesture of peace. "I don't know. He seemed legit."

"Okay. So what did he suggest you do?"

"He said there's an airfield in La Spezia. It's rarely used, but he has a team on board a Boeing C-17 Globemaster III set to land there within the hour. He gave me the address. If I can meet him there, he'll debrief me once we're in the air."

"Globemaster III." She said the name of the aircraft wistfully. "That sounds like a big airplane."

Sam nodded, surprised by his instinctive knowledge on aircraft. "Yeah, it's the largest aircraft in the US Air Force's transport fleet."

"Do they know it's a grass runway? Can it even land on grass?"

Sam grinned. "You bet it can. The Boeing C-17 Globemaster III is practically a tank with wings. It can fly, land, and takeoff again anywhere it pleases."

"That's good." Her voice softened. "So, you're leaving my life again."

"Yeah. But not for long. I'll get everything ironed out, and then I'll give you a call and we can catch up properly… if you're okay with that?"

She wrote down her cell number. "I've waited this long just to talk to you. I'd love to meet up again once your memory's back…" Her eyes drifted downward. "That is, if you still want to, after your memory comes back."

He squeezed her hand affectionately. "Hey, you've saved me from a lot of trouble. Without you, I might have been killed by the Russian mafia, or whoever the hell it is that wants me dead… so I think it's safe to say I owe you my life. Trust me, I'll make time to see you as soon as this is all sorted out and I have my memory back."

"Promise?"

"Promise."

She suppressed a frown. "So, you're still in the marines?"

Sam grinned. "It looks like it."

Chapter Twenty-Five

Pentagon Operations Center

The secretary of defense paced the operations room.

It was taking longer than she had expected and hoped for Sam Reilly to show up. It seemed impossible to believe that after all the man had been through, he could have drowned simply jumping into the ocean.

She had played out the series of unfortunate events that had led them to Sam's catastrophic position. There had been more than a dozen possible outcomes, but in none of them, or in her wildest dreams, did jumping into the calm waters of the Tyrrhenian Sea and drowning appear.

Her personal cell phone rang.

Few people had direct access to her.

She took a couple steps to the empty end of the room and accepted the call. "Yes?"

It was Tom Bower. "What the hell went wrong?"

She paused. Took a deep breath. It wasn't like Tom to lose his control. If she let him go too much further, he might just take everything past the point of no return. "Excuse me?"

"You said you would protect him!"

"I did, and I will… to the best of my abilities."

"No. That's not what you said before. You said you'd get him out of it!"

"I did… or at least I've tried my best. Good God, Tom, you know he's my best operative, and one of my closest allies. The last thing I wanted to see was Sam get killed. That's why I took the risk in the first place and tried to get him out of it. Do you think I would have tried, if I had any other options left to me?"

That gave Tom some pause. He knew the truth. "Then who the hell screwed it up?"

"It doesn't matter whose mistake it was. The fact is, we're at the location where we're at, and now we need to work out what to do about it – if anything can be done."

"No," Tom's voice was emphatic. "I need to know, who screwed up!"

The secretary of defense exhaled. "You're not going to like the truth."

"Don't give me that. I deserve to know. We're talking about my closest friend. So I'm going to ask you again, who screwed up?"

She nodded to herself, certain that Tom wouldn't be dismissed easily. "Sam Reilly did."

"How?"

"When we erased his memory, we had no idea his instincts would kick in… he was supposed to be taken into protective custody by the Italian police and charged with murder until we were able to get this whole mess sorted out."

"So what went wrong?"

"We didn't take into account that Sam's instincts, developed over a lifetime of overcoming life and death challenges, were sharp. They couldn't be subdued like his memories, which were so easily wiped clean."

Tom said, "He ran…"

"Yes."

"And the others?"

"They tried to catch him… but, Sam's instincts kicked in again…"

Tom's voice showed a wry sense of pleasure. "How many were killed?"

"Two… that we know of. Possibly three."

"It was a mistake to think you could control the situation."

"Listen here, Tom Bower, I did control the scene. I tipped the Italian police chief to be there. We mobilized a SEAL team… and besides, you yourself were there to retrieve him if things went wrong."

Tom said, "So then, if you had everything under control, why did I just get a phone call from Sam saying that he'd nearly been killed?"

"You did?" she said, excitedly. "He's alive?"

"Yes. No thanks to you!"

"Where is he now?"

"I don't know. An ex-girlfriend's place, still within Vernazza."

"All right, we'll send a retrieval team in to bring him out now!"

"I told him we could have the Globemaster III with a team on board on a disused airstrip on La Spezia."

"And he will be there?"

"He'll be there. Will our team be there in time?"

She mentally checked where the aircraft would be by now. It was circling the coast of Cinque Terra. It wouldn't take them long to get clearance to land at La Spezia. If Sam could reach them, she would make sure they were in there to greet him. "Yes. They will be there."

"Good. Don't screw it up this time."

The secretary of defense bit back at his insolence. He was a good friend of Sam Reilly's, and was understandably agitated. She didn't try to reprimand him for it. "One more thing, Tom."

"What?"

"Is he armed?"

Tom thought about that seriously. He sighed. "No. I don't think so."

"Good. I wouldn't like to think of him inadvertently killing one of his own."

"No. But then again, I don't like to consider what would happen if one of the others reach him first."

"How could they?" The Secretary asked. "Nobody knows where he is."

"All right, Genevieve and I will head into town, just to keep a look out while he gets out."

The Secretary frowned. "Is that really a good idea?"

"Probably not. But I'm not taking chances this time round."

"Okay. Good luck."

The Secretary ended the call.

Craig Martin, the director of the CIA, a heavyset man with a surly disposition, approached her. He wore an expression of mulish obstinacy. "Any news, Madam Secretary?"

She nodded. "He's staying at an ex-girlfriend's house in Vernazza."

The lines in his face deepened. "Do we know who the girl is?"

"Yes. It's Dr. Catarina Marcello."

"Good God! That can't be a coincidence."

"It would be highly unlikely."

Martin grimaced. "So he knows the truth then?"

"I don't think so. He just contacted Tom Bower. Said he'd found the contact details online. He's got no memory and he's terrified of who he might be."

"The question is, what are we going to do about it? If he's gotten this far already it won't take him long to put the rest of it together."

She exhaled a deep breath between pursed lips. "I agree. The window's narrowing. How much time have we got?"

Craig Martin glanced at his wristwatch. "Fifty-six hours."

She swallowed. "It will be close."

"What have you done about it?"

The Secretary said, "We've dispatched a SEAL team to retrieve him."

The director frowned. "Won't our involvement get traced back to us?"

"No. This is a wet team. They're designed to be separate. A cut off switch so no one can trace them back to us."

"All right. Let's just hope they reach him in time."

Chapter Twenty-Six

Andre finished drying himself with a towel.

A rapidly growing team of police detectives shot him questions in rapid fire succession about the ghost ship and specifically, how the police chief was abducted. After all, it wasn't every day that a dilapidated shipwreck kidnaps the chief of police, before coming alive and racing off at the speed of a jetboat.

The lead detective asked, "Have you ever seen anything like it?"

Andre raised his eyebrows. "The ghost ship?"

"Yeah. A ship that looks like a wreck only to be equipped with high powered hydrojet engines, capable of coming alive at a moment's notice."

Andre thought about it, not sure how much he was willing to disclose. He made a suppressed smile. Nodded. "They're called ghost ships. Interpol is constantly searching for them. They look like rust buckets, soon to be shipwrecks, but have powerful engines and high-tech satellite connection."

"For what purpose?"

"They travel around the world, setting up untraceable, illegal, and highly dangerous marketplaces on the dark web."

"You're talking about the part of the internet that isn't indexed, making it impossible to find on any search engine?"

"No. That's the deep web. There's nothing illegal about the deep web and plenty of mainstream websites exist in the deep web. The content of the deep web is hidden behind HTTP encryptions and passwords, and includes many very common uses such as web mail, online banking, and services that users must pay for, and which are protected by paywalls, such as video on demand and some online magazines and newspapers."

"And the dark web?" the detective asked.

"That's different. The internet, you see, is split into three different levels. At the top you have the surface web, a place accessible by anyone with a web browser and a search engine. But it's just the tip of the iceberg. Below it is the deep web, which is estimated to contain up to ninety percent of the world's internet data. This is where banking, legal documents, scientific reports, universities, and even social media exist. And way down, below all of that, is the dark web."

"Where criminals sell their wares in plain sight."

"Exactly. The dark web is a collection of websites that exist on an encrypted network and cannot be found by using traditional search engines or visited by using traditional browsers. Almost all sites on the so-called Dark Web hide their identity using the Tor encryption tool. It exists on darknets, overlay networks that use the Internet but require specific software, configurations, or authorization to access.The darknets which constitute the dark web include small, friend-to-friend, peer-to-peer networks, as well as large, popular networks like Tor, Freenet, I2P, and Riffle operated by public organizations and individuals."

"What about the ghost ship?"

"The ghost ship is used to access and maintain specific, most likely highly illegal marketplaces, on the dark web." Andre took a breath. "The data stored inside here might be worth a fortune to Interpol. It's a positive goldmine of criminal information. Crime syndicates are willing to spend a fortune to protect information like this. That's why they use ghost ships. The idea is, if their connection is somehow breached, or their physical location identified, they merely pull the plug, and send the ship straight to the bottom."

The detective closed his notebook. "Thank you for your help, Mr. Dufort. I'm sure my people will be in touch with your people shortly. We'll let you know if we locate the ghost ship and, likewise, expect you to share any information you receive."

Andre shook the detective's hand. "You have my word."

He headed back to the apartment that he'd rented.

Inside he took out a secure satellite phone and dialed a number from memory.

A man answered on the first ring. "Yes?"

"It's done. The man's dead. But… there's something else you're not going to like."

"What?"

"Sam Reilly wasn't the only person to come off the Ghost Ship."

The man on the other end of the line replied, "He wasn't?"

"No. There was a dead girl in the rowboat with him."

"Strange."

"It gets worse. I knew the woman. She was my other target. I killed her three days ago."

The line went silent for a few seconds, as the man on the other end mulled it over. He said, "But that was nowhere near here. Hell, it wasn't even on the same damned continent!"

Andre nodded. "I know, I know…"

"What the hell does that even mean?"

Andre swallowed hard. "It means someone else knew about the contract, and they're leaving me a dangerous message."

"Yeah?" The man on the other end of the line said. "Well I've got a message for you. Sam Reilly's best friend, Tom Bower, just called the Secretary of Defense. It appears your dead man's still walking. What's more, the Secretary of Defense has agreed to send a team in to retrieve him as we speak."

"Do you know where from?"

"They're landing at a small airstrip in La Spezia and Sam Reilly's going to make his own way there."

Andre grinned. "Then I'll just have to make sure to beat him there."

Chapter Twenty-Seven

Fifty-Two Hours

Sam asked, "Do you have a car here?"

Catarina frowned. "I don't have one. But you can borrow my motorcycle."

"You ride a bike?"

"Always have. Don't you remember?" She smiled. "Of course, you don't remember."

Sam grinned. "Can I ride it?"

"Sure." She grabbed a set of keys and passed them to him. "Go for it."

He smiled. "No. I mean, do I know how to ride it?"

She nodded. "Yeah. You can ride a motorcycle all right."

"Thanks." Sam paused. "I don't think I can get it back to you. I'll leave it somewhere near the airstrip at La Spezia. Is there any way you'll be able to reach it?"

"Yeah. There's a secret key safe beneath the fuel tank. Just make sure you leave the keys there and I'll come pick it up in the morning."

"Thanks. Really, I mean it."

"You're welcome." She smiled. "Come on, I'll walk you to where it's parked. What are you going to do about the suitcase?"

"Good question. I forgot about that. I can't exactly carry it on the motorcycle."

"Wait here, I have a backpack you can have."

Sam smiled. "Thanks. Again. I'll get it back to you if I manage to survive."

Catarina returned a few seconds later with a small backpack. Sam opened the suitcase and quickly transferred its contents into the backpack. He zipped up the backpack and threw it over his shoulders, making sure to connect and tighten the waist straps.

Sam opened the door and stepped outside.

It was heading into midafternoon. He breathed deeply, taking in the warm sea breeze. It felt good. He felt good. Things were far from making sense, but at least they were coming together. He had been on a mission when something went wrong. Someone intentionally erased his memory. Whoever that was, and why, could still be worked out. The important thing was that he would be meeting Tom Bower soon and would learn the truth.

He held Catarina's hand affectionately as he strolled down the masonry path and stairs that meandered down to the roadway behind the set of buildings. He forced himself to stroll, taking on the appearance of a romantic couple on vacation, instead of a fugitive on the run for his life.

They reached the bottom of the stairs, turned east onto *Via M. Caratino*, making their way through the narrow street, heading uphill toward the city's communal carpark.

Far behind them, and still high up on the masonry steps, back where they had come from, two people began to follow them. One was a big guy, the other a woman. He couldn't make out a lot from the distance. But even at a glance, both moved with the speed and agility of professional soldiers. They might have been walking to catch a bus, but had that been the case, there was no reason for them to pick up speed and purpose, as soon as they had spotted him.

They were making a beeline straight for him.

No. One thing was certain, whoever they were, they were after him.

Sam's eyes darted between his pursuers and Catarina. "Don't suppose they're friends of yours?"

"Afraid not. Any chance they might be yours?"

"Not a chance in hell. Tom Bower said that he'd meet me on the aircraft."

"Then I suggest we get a move on."

"Agreed. How much farther to your bike?"

"Not far. Come on, we'll cut through this alleyway to the main street."

Sam followed Catarina as they both picked up their pace to a run. Behind them, the big guy and the girl started to run.

Catarina said, "Through here!"

"I see it!" Sam said, as they ducked beneath a sandstone archway, cutting across the back of the *Pizzeria Lercari Ercole* – a pizza restaurant – and turned right onto *Via Roma*.

They entered the main street. Sam forced himself to slow to a fast walk to try to avoid drawing too much attention to them.

He scanned the *Via Roma* as they headed uphill.

The last train had left more than an hour ago, leaving the city nearly tourist free and almost deserted compared to the throng of people in the street earlier in the day.

To their left, they passed an old man parked on the side of the cobbled street. He was struggling to get his ascot green, 1972 Lancia Montecarlo Coupe started. Like everyone else who visited or lived in the small coastal village of Vernazza, he'd probably left the car as soon as he'd arrived, and was now suffering the consequence of its disuse. Behind them some polizia were walking briskly their way, coming from the harbor to the south. Up ahead, stationed at the entrance to the communal carpark, were two men loitering, wearing overcoats and smoking cigarettes.

There was no way any normal person would be wearing overcoats in Vernazza during its summer months.

Sam's eyes darted left to right.

He was searching for a way around the two most likely threats.

There were none.

He could turn around, but that meant dealing with the big guy and woman with him, who were clearly following them. It also meant they were more likely to be confronted by the polizia.

Catarina said, "Two o'clock. Do you see them?"

Sam kept moving. "I see them."

"They sure as hell don't look like they belong here."

"I agree," Sam said, without slowing his stride.

"What do you want to do about it?"

"I don't know. Something will come up."

She took a surreptitious glance behind her. The polizia had picked up their pace, the big guy and the woman were closing the gap. "We're running out of options. Do we keep going or turn around? It's your call."

"Keep going," Sam said, his voice emphatic. "We're going to have to deal with someone. May as well keep heading in the right direction while we do it."

"Okay. I hope you know what you're doing."

Sam grinned. "Not a clue, but I'm sure something will come up. It usually does."

"Oh yeah?" She arched her eyebrow. "That's very reassuring coming from a guy who's lost his memory."

Sam didn't make a response.

He kept walking past the two men in overcoats, through the sandstone arch, and into the underground carpark. He met the first man in the overcoat's eye and gave a firm nod as acknowledgement. There was instant recognition in the man's face, but no movement.

Sam gritted his teeth and kept walking.

The parking lot was underground.

They had only made it fifteen feet before the sound of trailing footsteps echoed behind them.

Sam turned to greet his attackers.

Both men had their handguns drawn. Glock 19s.

Sam reached for his handgun. But it was too late. The smaller of the two men said, "I wouldn't if I were you."

Sam paused, his hand just about on the weapon's handle. He relaxed his fingers so they came free, and distanced his hand from the weapon. The big guy behind him quickly removed the handgun and stepped back so that he wasn't close enough for Sam to reach.

"Good decision." The man closest to him said, "Now, Mr. Reilly, I think you'd better come with us."

Chapter Twenty-Eight

Sam turned the palms of his hands skyward. "Hey guys, do I know you?"

"No, but my boss knows you. He seems to think that you have something that belongs to him in that suitcase."

"This suitcase?" Catarina asked. "It's mine. There's nothing that belongs to your boss inside." She licked her lips. "Definitely nothing that he's ever going to get his hands on."

Sam made a quick observation of the two men, taking them in with a glance.

One was a big heavyset man with a thick, short, neck and a set of teeth full of gold. Next to him, the other man was smaller, but had a hard expression and a supercilious smile. Both looked like hardened criminals. Paid thugs. Professional bullies.

He grinned. "Hey, my memory must be coming back, I do know you two."

"Oh yeah?" said the man with golden teeth.

"Yeah, you're doctor evil in that old Bond film..." Sam turned his gaze to Gold Teeth. "And you're the villain's paid brute. The real dumb one if I remember correctly."

Catrina made a thin-lipped smile. "No, no, Sam... you've got it all wrong. Your memory's not getting any better."

Sam frowned. "It isn't? I was starting to get excited."

"Afraid not. You're mixing the James Bond films." Catarina made a coy smile and gestured toward the bigger of the two men. "This here is Jaws, the towering bad guy with steel teeth from *The Spy Who Loved Me*..." She made a point of studying the skinnier one. "And this one here... if I had to guess, is Doctor Dolittle!"

Sam opened his mouth, suppressed a smile. "So it is... so it is. The man who talks to animals."

Jaws bared his golden teeth, like a rabid dog. He turned the Glock on Catarina. "Hand over the suitcase, love… before we kill you as well as him."

Sam froze. His eyes darting between their two attackers, before landing on Catarina. Her jaw tightened and her eyes defiant, giving him a firm nod of approval.

The next seven seconds happened in a blur.

Catarina threw the metallic case at Jaws. It was heavy and solid. Thrown with a strong arm, it carried with it a surprisingly sinister amount of force. Jaws moved quickly for a man his size, stepping back, protecting his face with his arms.

Dr. Dolittle was the first to respond. He turned the barrel of his Glock 19 from its previous target of Sam Reilly, toward Catarina, and squeezed the trigger.

Catarina was already diving to the ground.

At the same time, Sam lunged toward Dr. Dolittle. Sam gripped his attacker's wrists, causing the shot to go wide.

Dr. Dolittle twisted his body, turning around in an attempt to pull his hand free of Sam's grip.

Sam shoved the man's arm downward in the opposite direction. The ulna and radius – those mostly parallel bones that ran the length of the forearm joined by a series of tendons and ligaments responsible for the wide range of movement of the wrists – were forced to twist apart. The trochlear notch, being the weakest point in the elbow, gave out first with a blood curdling SNAP!

Dr. Dolittle screamed in agony and dropped the handgun.

Sam reached down to grab it, but Dolittle, realizing that he was going to struggle to maintain control of the weapon, kicked it away with his foot.

Jaws leveled his weapon at Sam and said, "That's enough!"

Sam stood up, still holding Dolittle's broken arm. He positioned the man in front of him like a human shield.

"You think that little pissant's going to shield you from anything?" Jaws asked, his lips twisted in a malevolent grin. "I can kill both of you with the same bullet."

Dolittle shouted, "No!"

Jaws shrugged. "Sorry, boss. But we're both dead if we screw this up. And frankly, I never liked you anyway."

Dolittle cursed him in Russian.

And the underground carpark was filled with gunshots.

Chapter Twenty-Nine

Lookout, overlooking Vernazza

Andre gave one last glance at the harbor of Vernazza.

He thanked the detectives who had given him a lift out of the main part of the city, where few cars were allowed access. He unlocked his rental car, which he'd left at a public carpark, and walked the rest of the way into the city the day before.

A moment later, he heard the sound of multiple shots fired. The polizia heard them too.

Andre watched them quickly climb back into the police car, switch on their flashing lights and wailing siren, and disappear into the medieval city.

Andre toyed with the idea of going back just to be certain, but immediately dismissed the idea. No, either Sam Reilly was as good as he'd been led to believe and he would make his way to the rendezvous, or he wasn't and he was already under arrest by the polizia.

Either way, it wasn't going to help him to return to Sam Reilly.

Andre grinned at his surprisingly worthy adversary, making a silent prayer that the man would manage to evade the polizia, and reach the rendezvous point.

He sat down in the cramped Fiat, turned the ignition, and began to make his way to the location to beat him there.

Chapter Thirty

Sam looked across the room.

Jaws was lying dead on the ground. Blood weeping from three bullet holes in his chest.

Sam's eyes drifted to the left, where Catarina still held the Glock.

Dr. Dolittle shifted his position, dislocating his elbow further in the processes, but came free with a painful grunt.

Sam didn't try to catch him.

Dolittle turned and ran toward the end of the carpark.

He made it about five feet, before Catarina fired two more rounds into the back of his head.

Sam swore. "Was that really necessary?"

Catarina bit her lower lip, her hands still shaking. "I don't know. Honestly, I think I now understand what you meant when you said that you reacted earlier on instinct alone – letting that kill or be killed thing kick in."

Sam said, "He was making a run for it."

She dismissed his complaint. "Yeah, probably to get his friends and finish off whatever the hell you started. Come on, I'll show you my bike before the polizia arrive."

"Good idea." Sam bent down and picked up the Makarov semiautomatic, tucking it into the crease in his back once more. His eyes looked to Catarina. "You have somewhere to dispose of that?"

Her gaze went distant. "I'll think of something."

They followed the underground carpark down a series of stairs to the bottom, where an obsidian black, Ducati Diavel sports cruiser was waiting for them.

Sam grinned. "That's your bike?"

"Yeah, what did you think I'd ride?"

"I don't know. But it's a hell of a nice bike."

"Thanks. I like it."

He straddled the seat, inserted the key, and pressed the ignition button. The powerful 1198cc Testastretta 11 Degree DS engine was an assertion of power and fluidity. It produced 152 horsepower and 123 Newton-meters of torque. It felt powerful just to sit on.

Catarina said, "You'd better go."

Sam frowned. "You're not coming with me?"

She shook her head. Her lovely dark eyes were solemn. "No. It's better if I stay here. I'll only slow you down."

"What about the polizia?"

She suppressed a smile. "I'll deal with them."

"They might arrest you!"

"I doubt it. Just because I walked in here with you doesn't mean that we were together. I'll just say that I came to pick up something from a friend."

Sam took a breath. "Are you sure?"

"Yeah. I'll be fine. They might have seen us walking near each other, but there's nothing they can hold me for. Just go."

"All right." Sam revved the engine. "Wait… I don't want to lose you again."

"Then don't."

He smiled. "When this is all over, I promise I'll find you again!"

She kissed him on the lips. "You'd better."

Sam placed her dark helmet on, covering his face. He revved the engine, dropped the clutch, and with screeching tires, he took off up the series of ramps, and onto *Strada Provinciale 61*– the only road out of Vernazza.

Chapter Thirty-One

Tom watched the obsidian black Ducati sports cruiser race out of the carpark.

The Polizia surrounded the carpark, getting ready to breech it.

Tom exhaled. Sam had made it out just in time. "See, Genevieve, even without his memory Sam's resourceful as hell. He'll be in La Spezia in fifteen minutes."

"I give him ten minutes on that bike."

"You might be right. I'll call the pilot, make sure they're ready to take off." He picked up his cell phone and pressed redial on his last call. It rang out. He frowned. Tried a second secure number. It just kept ringing.

Genevieve met his eye. "What is it?"

"The Globemaster III's been compromised!"

Her face made an incredulous grimace. "How? I thought it was guarded by a team of SEALs?"

"No. Most of them were already on their way here. There's only a skeleton crew on board. They weren't expecting company."

Genevieve said, "What do you want to do about? Are you going to contact the Secretary of Defense?"

"No. That's the only person who knew where Sam was heading…"

"You think the Secretary betrayed Sam?"

"I doubt it, but one thing's for certain, she's compromised his position."

Genevieve nodded. It made sense. Tom had called the Secretary and said they were headed to the rendezvous point at the airfield at La Spezia, and now the Globemaster III had been compromised. "Okay, so we need to intercept Sam before he gets there. Do you have any idea how we're going to catch him without transport?"

Tom glanced at the ascot green Lancia Montecarlo. It was the only car in the street. An old man had stepped out of it, lifted the hood, and was trying to persuade its engine to start. "Yeah, I think I've got an idea…"

Chapter Thirty-Two

Tom stared at the car.

The Pininfarina designed – and built – two-door Lancia Montecarlo was a rear-wheel drive, mid-engined, two-seater sports car. Montecarlos were available as fixed head "Coupés" and also as "Spiders" with solid A and B pillars, but a large flat folding canvas roof between them.

This one was a Spider with the top down, and it looked beautiful.

Tom's father had owned an American version of the identical car when he was growing up. It was badged as *The Scorpion*, since General Motors had already used the name Monte Carlo for one of their other cars.

With each turn of the ignition the piston would fire, struggle, and eventually conk out as the twin exhaust pipes spat out near-blue exhaust fumes.

Tom grinned.

The owner had left the manual choke out, starving the carburetor of air, and causing it to stall.

Tom gestured to the owner, "May I try?"

The old man's face took on a puzzled expression.

Tom said, "I'm a mechanic... I help..."

The Italian man threw his hands down with a wave. "It's no good..."

Tom climbed in, disengaged the choke, and turned the ignition. The starter motor turned, but the engine failed to fire.

He frowned.

Genevieve said, "I thought you were good with cars."

"Yeah, so did I."

The Italian cursed. Some words, Tom reflected, were universal no matter what language they were spoken in.

He gave it another try.

This time the engine caught, and roared into life.

Genevieve opened the passenger side door and climbed in.

The owner waved his arms and shouted at them. "What are you doing?"

Tom said, "I'm sorry… we'll bring it back… I promise!"

The owner blocked them from leaving by standing in their way.

Tom said to Genevieve, "I don't know how to speak Italian… do you know anything that might get us out of here?"

"Leave it to me."

"You speak Italian?"

She grinned. "A little."

Genevieve withdrew her Israeli Uzi and gestured it toward the old man.

The Italian dived out of the way.

Tom dropped the handbrake, released the clutch, and floored the accelerator.

The Lancia Montecarlo raced off.

Tom turned to Genevieve. "We just stole a man's car and you threaten him with an Uzi?"

She shrugged. "Hey, it got him out of our way didn't it?"

"Yeah… but…"

She dismissed his tone. "We're doing this to save Sam's life, remember?"

"And that makes it okay?"

She grinned. "You bet it does."

Chapter Thirty-Three

Catarina gripped the metallic suitcase and moved quickly, exiting the carpark onto the back of *Via Visconti.*

She heard shouting coming from the Polizia who cordoned off the carpark, slowly stopping anyone from entering or leaving.

She headed south, toward her apartment.

Nearly five hundred feet along the narrow, cobblestone street, she heard the footsteps of someone behind her begin to follow.

She kept walking.

On the third corner, she turned and was greeted by two polizia officers.

"Stop right there."

She stopped suddenly. "Yes officer?"

"We have reason to believe that you're carrying that suitcase for a known criminal."

"This suitcase?" She looked alluringly startled, mouth open, eyes wide. "I don't know what you mean, this is mine."

"I'm sorry, but we're going to have to get you to prove that."

"I don't see how. It's not like I carry a receipt around with me for it…"

The police officer wore an expression of mulish obstinacy. "Just open the damned case."

"Hey, no reason to be rude, I haven't done anything wrong."

The second officer, eager to please, said, "It's all right, we're just doing our duty, ma'am. There's a violent criminal on the loose. He was seen carrying a suitcase that looked identical to that last night. So, if you don't mind, we're going to have to get you to open it."

She drew a breath. Her face was set with an expression of embarrassment. "Okay, if I must."

Catarina put in the code, unlocked the suitcase and opened it to reveal nothing but sexy Italian lingerie.

The police officer's eyes went wide, their faces flushed, but their eyes turned away.

"I'm sorry, ma'am."

Chapter Thirty-Four

Strada Provinciale 61 was the only way out of Vernazza by road.

It was a steep, narrow, winding, and altogether dangerous road that meandered its way in sharp twists and turns over the heavily terraced landscape.

The Ducati Diavel hugged the road like a heat seeking missile, intent on tracking its target. Its powerful engine purred through the corners, celebrating a cacophony of exhaust sounds as Sam Reilly rapidly took the bike up and down through its gears. With its horsepower and torque, the bike eagerly climbed the steep hills without hesitation.

He had to work to restrain himself from picking up too much speed and letting the Italian sports bike run away from him. His eyes remained glued on the speedometer, paying meticulous attention to avoid drawing attention to himself. The last thing he needed now was to get pulled over by the Polizia for speeding.

He leaned into two back to back hairpin turns, his knees mere inches away from the blacktop below. On the second one, he straightened the bike upright, and jammed on the brakes hard – because up ahead, the traffic had come to a complete stop.

His heart pounded as he brought the Ducati to a standstill.

In a coastal hamlet that restricted the use of vehicles to local residents and government cars, it seemed impossible to believe that three cars had amounted to enough traffic to come to a complete stop.

Up ahead was a single workman, holding a stop sign. With bureaucratic authority the man's face was plastered with obstinacy, as though he alone had the power to stop all traffic, despite there being no obvious work being done on a perfectly good piece of road. The road worker's eyes seemed to scan the occupants of each car, meeting the various drivers with a dogged challenge, searching and daring them to defy his authority.

The place could have been getting its annual resurfacing, but it seemed unlikely. For one thing, the road surface seemed good, with the blacktop smooth and absent of any potholes. Secondly, even if there was roadwork going on – as the man with the stop sign suggested – the question remained, where were the workers?

At the front of the queue was a police officer on a motorcycle.

Sam swallowed hard and tried to shrink his shoulders back behind the Ducati's large fuel tank, while reminding himself that the police were looking for a man with a metallic suitcase, not someone riding an obsidian colored motorcycle. Besides, with Catarina's matching obsidian helmet, he doubted very much that anyone would be looking at him.

The second vehicle in the line was a Mercedes-Benz G-Class. The "G" was short for Geländewagen, which meant "cross country vehicle." The light truck looked like a jarring contradiction of purposes – on one hand it looked like a go-anywhere truck built to withstand the harshness of the most rugged terrains, while on the other, it was the ultimate statement of class and luxury.

This one was a G63 AMG, a special edition limited to 2002 and the only model with a 6.3 liter V12 engine.

The windows were tinted, preventing Sam from seeing the occupants inside, but already, his gut told him if there was to be an ambush, it would most likely come from whoever was inside the G63. The light truck was priced well above a quarter of a million dollars, in any currency. People with that kind of money bought supercars – hell, in Italy, someone with that sort of money to burn, would surely buy a Ferrari, Lamborghini, or Pagani – unless they wanted to make a different sort of statement? Something like, we're a hell of a lot tougher than you.

And who wants to achieve that impression?

Drug dealers, heads of organized crime, and…

Members of the Russian mafia.

Sam revved the Ducati's throttle, his eyes scanning for a way around the two cars if he had to make a move. It all depended on where the ambush came from. The bike was fast, but hardly fast enough to outrun a bullet if he was attacked.

If it came from whoever was in the Mercedes in front of him, he would have only a split second to make a decision. Life or death would rest on his ability to accelerate away as soon as one of those doors opened.

In his mirrors, a fourth vehicle pulled up behind him.

It was an old Italian car. Sam recognized it as a Lancia Montecarlo. The convertible version, with the top down. This one had been recently painted Ascot Green, making it appear somewhat modern, despite Sam placing the vehicle's age as somewhere around the 1970s.

In the back of his mind, something seemed familiar about the car.

He'd seen it back in Vernazza.

But it wasn't just that. He remembered, somewhere in the deep recess of his subconscious at the time, thinking that there was something about it. It was a distant memory. More like something from his youth. Maybe his own father had owned one? Although, from what he'd read about his father, the car wasn't quite up to his taste in exotic and expensive cars.

If not his father, then who?

Tom Bower's father.

That was it! The first memory to return from his past. It was a childhood memory. His friend's father had owned one. It would have been old, even then, and it wasn't green, it was red… but all the same, the car had been Tom's father's!

Sam felt elated to have made such a recollection. It confirmed Catarina's theory that parts of his memory would come back, albeit slowly, and more likely older memories than recent experiences.

The thought about Tom jolted another understanding.

His eyes fixed on the driver and passenger of the Montecarlo.

Back in Vernazza, there had been an old Italian man struggling to start the car, but the driver in it now looked young. The Lancia Montecarlo was unique, too recognizable to be mistaken for another car, and much too unlikely that there were simply two of them.

No, the old Italian man had gotten out, and two new people had gotten in since Sam had walked past the car back in Vernazza.

Sam's eyes narrowed as he glanced at the two occupants in his mirrors.

One male and one female. The man was a good head taller than the woman, with giant shoulders, and a carefree grin on his face. The woman had short, brown hair, and an impish face. He recognized the girl from the pictures of the crew on board the *Tahila* that he'd seen on the internet, although he couldn't put a name to her.

If one of his crew was in the passenger seat, who was the driver?

His eyes locked with the driver's.

The man showed recognition, giving him a firm, almost friendly nod.

Sam had seen that look before.

He knew where he'd seen that face before, too. He exhaled a deep sigh of relief.

It was Tom Bower.

An instant later, two doors from the Mercedes G63 opened – and the ambush began.

Chapter Thirty-Five

Sam dropped the clutch.

It was like releasing the reins of a thoroughbred. The Ducati Diavel shot forward. The driver of the Mercedes was the first to respond. In a split second, two things happened simultaneously. The driver of the Mercedes drew his handgun – leveling its barrel at Sam – and the Ducati's front wheel lifted high off the ground.

The sound of multiple shots rang in Sam's ears.

Sparks flew off the underside of the motorcycle, turning the metallic, obsidian paint, into a series of fiery shards. An instant later, the Ducati's front wheel slammed into the driver's open side door, slamming it shut and crushing the driver in the metal doorframe with a sickening crunch.

The front wheel dropped to the ground.

Sam balanced the bike, working to keep it from flipping. He straightened it, opened the throttle all the way up, and shot through the gap between the roadworker and the two police bikes. The roadworker dropped his stop sign, trading it for a pistol, which he immediately aimed at Sam.

The fake roadworker never got a chance to take a shot.

Instead, his body was sprayed with bullets – either intentionally shot by Tom or the woman with him, the thugs in the Mercedes, or even accidentally by the police. He couldn't tell. In fact, there was little he could discern about who was attacking him or who was defending him – if anyone.

One thing was certain. Sam wasn't going to wait around to find out who wanted him dead or alive. He accelerated hard into the first corner, glad to be out of a direct line of sight of anyone who was trying to shoot him.

Behind him, he heard the sirens of police motorcycles in pursuit.

The road forked in two directions – north and south.

Sam turned right, heading south toward La Spezia on *Strada Provinciale 51*. If *Strada Provinciale 61* was dangerous, *Strada Provinciale 51* was outright lethal on a motorcycle. The narrow road snaked backward and forward through sharp doglegs and hairpin turns as it negotiated the series of terraced olive groves and vineyards along Cinque Terra.

The Polizia rode BMW R1200RTs. They were more powerful and faster on the straights, but less agile on the infinite corners, resulting in a kind of shuffle whereby any gains they made would be lost on the corners, but retaken on the straights.

Sam rode hard, dipping into the corners at speeds that nearly forced him to graze his knees in the process.

At first, the three competing riders appeared equally paced, but with time, the Polizia were reducing the gap. Whatever advantage Sam had by riding the sportier Ducati, was lost over time by the fact that he'd never ridden *Strada Provinciale 51* before and the Polizia had.

They passed Riomaggiore, the last city of Cinque Terra, and entered a series of steep bends, heading down into the coastal region of La Spezia.

Sam glanced at the two Polizia riders in his mirrors.

They were close enough now that he could almost reach out and touch them. Definitely close enough to get shot, not that he expected the Polizia to take one at him while they were on bikes. Contrary to whatever Hollywood might have people believe, shooting and riding a motorcycle at high speed through sharp bends was never going to happen.

So, if they weren't trying to get close enough to shoot him, what were they trying to do?

Sam swallowed.

Could it be they were trying to set up a road block? It was possible they were carrying road spikes. It wasn't like he could turn around now. The bikes were all faster than the Mercedes and the Lancia, but no doubt, neither of them would be far behind – and he still wasn't sure that Tom Bower was on his side.

The rider tried to cut him off at the next corner.

The curve looked like it went forever. He entered it at speed, unable to see where it eventually came out. He dropped down another gear, leaned into the curve, and accelerated hard. Behind him, the Polizia rode his BMW like a professional superbike rider on the track.

The turn ended and Sam straightened the Ducati up and brought it up another gear.

In his mirror, he watched the BMW swing to the right and the left, as though its rider was judging the best location to overtake.

Sam entered the next curve, cutting it as close to the inside edge as he dared. He really felt like he was competing at the superbike grand prix, only in this case, he wasn't competing for wealth, accolades, and glory – he was competing for his life.

As the corner straightened, the BMW rider swerved to the opposite end of the road, putting the most amount of room between the two of them that he'd had for some time.

Sam frowned.

A moment later, he knew exactly why.

The other rider, having ridden the route daily, instinctively knew the line – and right now, the curve was about to turn in the opposite direction, back in on itself.

Sam cursed, and swerved to the left, trying to close the gap.

He dismissed any caution and cut the corner so short, that his wheels were mere inches away from coming off the blacktop and onto the grass.

The BMW had matched him, leaning in beside him.

Sam couldn't keep it up. It was now or never.

He swerved the bike to the right.

The BMW rider tried to straighten up.

Both bikes locked together for a split second.

Sam shoved his boot on the BMW's handlebars and kicked.

The Polizia tried to regain control. He was a good rider, but there was nothing he could do about it. The front wheel had locked up, and the bike was on an unavoidable collision course with the ground. The rider dropped the bike, and slid off into the grass beside the road.

Sam straightened up and set up for the next corner.

He gave one parting glance in his mirrors and saw that the Polizia had stopped sliding and was already standing up again. The officer brushed himself off and picked up his radio mike.

Sam entered the next corner, and lost sight of his pursuers.

He kept the speed up, trying to attain as much distance as he could between himself and whatever pursuers still remained.

Sam was starting to feel confident. He'd lost sight of any pursuers and was certain he was still gaining more.

As soon as he could get off the main road he would.

Strada Provinciale delle Cinque Terra entered the underground tunnel beneath the national park leading into La Spezia.

The airstrip was close.

He was close.

And then he jammed on the brakes.

Because up ahead – at the end of the tunnel – a strip of metal barbs three inches wide known as stingers lined the entire width of the tunnel.

The device was used to deflate and shred tires.

They had been in use in the form of a caltrop – the anti-cavalry and anti-personnel versions being used as early as 331 BC by Darius III against Alexander the Great at the Battle of Gaugamela in Persia.

And now, they were about to make his day turn really shitty.

Sam kicked the bike back into gear, planted his right foot hard on the ground, and turned the bike about face, its rear tire screeching.

He accelerated hard the way he had come.

In the back of his mind, he tried to picture *Via Fabia Filzi* – the old way to La Spezia, replaced by the tunnel.

Chapter Thirty-Six

Tom frowned. "Well, that could have gone better."

Genevieve gave an indifferent half-shrug. "Hey, he's alive, isn't he?"

"You're right, it could have gone worse."

Tom tried to extract every single horsepower from the Lancia Montecarlo's 2.0 L Lampredi I4 engine as he navigated the sharp corners and steep gradients of *Strada Provinciale delle Cinque Terra*. The small engine, despite its age, seemed to revel in the challenge.

Behind them, the Mercedes G63 was picking up speed.

There was no way in the world they could outrun it. Forty years of engineering advancements was hard to compete against, even if the Mercedes was a four-wheel drive, weighing more than two tons. The Montecarlo was never going to beat it.

Tom asked, "You got a plan, Genevieve?"

"Yeah, drive faster."

Tom grinned. "Hey, I'm trying… but it's not going to happen."

"All right, all right… leave it to me."

"How?"

Genevieve bit her lower lip. "I don't know yet, I'll think of something. Just don't let it drive over us!"

Tom took the next corner in a diagonal line that would make some Formula One drivers panic. He got away with it, but knew he wouldn't be so lucky much longer. He shot a quick glance at Genevieve. "I'd be most obliged to you, darling, if you were to think a little faster."

"I'm working on it."

"Can't you just shoot the damned driver?"

Genevieve laughed. "Are you kidding me? A car like that… the owner would be getting ripped off if he – or she – didn't insist on complimentary bullet-resistant glass."

"You don't know that for certain, do you?"

"It's a pretty good guess," Genevieve replied.

They entered a long straight stretch.

The specialized edition V12 ate it up.

"Genevieve!" Tom yelled.

Genevieve aimed the Israeli Uzi and squeezed the trigger.

A burst of 9mm parabellums struck the windshield directly in front of the driver of the Mercedes. Small fractures in the glass, turned to splintered stars, in a tight grouping that would make the best marksmen proud, but the windshield remained intact.

Tom glanced in his rearview mirror. His lips curled into a suppressed grin. "It looks like they might have bullet resistant glass."

"Oh yeah, you think?" Genevieve replied.

Tom didn't bite. "What's next?"

"I suggest you get off the road as fast as you can."

"That's the best you've got?"

"That's all I've got."

"Can't you shoot its tires?"

"Sure, but it won't do anything to stop the Mercedes," Genevieve countered. "Those are run flat tires. I could shoot at them all day and the damned thing would keep moving."

The Mercedes G63 slammed into the back of them.

Tom worked the steering wheel, trying to keep the car from flipping off the side of the road, into the terraced landscape below.

Behind them, the Mercedes slowed.

Tom won the battle for control of the Montecarlo, finally ending the spin, facing the opposite direction from which he'd started.

The Mercedes drove right at them.

Tom planted his foot on the accelerator, locked the wheel full right, and turned into a private driveway.

The Mercedes didn't stop.

It drove past them, continuing its pursuit of Sam Reilly.

Tom reversed down the driveway, back onto *Strada Provinciale delle Cinque Terra* and continued his journey south to La Spezia.

Genevieve glanced at him. "Nice driving."

"Thanks."

"You know you're not going to catch up with Sam, right?"

"I know. I'm hoping we don't. Otherwise it means Sam's come off his bike. But just in case, I want to follow him all the way to the airstrip."

"Good idea."

Tom's cell phone rang. He picked it up. Listened and thanked the person on the other side.

Genevieve took one look at his expression and asked, "What is it?"

"That was Gabriele Valentino."

"Who?"

"The Italian Police Chief who you accidentally abducted."

Her face tightened. "Hey, it was dark. Besides, we put him back, and told him what was happening. Hell, his own boss had signed off on the project. No harm no foul, right?"

"Right."

"So what did he say?"

"The plan didn't work. They set up a line of road spikes across the *Strada Provinciale delle Cinque Terra* tunnel."

"What did Sam do?"

"He turned around."

"Ah shit... he's going to try and get to the airstrip through the second route, isn't he?"

"Yeah... you wrote it down before, what was its name?"

"Via Fabia Filzi."

"That's right."

Tom pulled his handbrake and swung the Montecarlo round in a single movement, before exchanging the brake for the accelerator again.

He swore loudly.

Genevieve asked, "What?"

"Sam's still heading for the original rendezvous point!"

Realization dawned on her face. "Oh shit!"

"It's all over if Sam boards that aircraft!"

Genevieve loaded a new magazine into her Uzi. Her face was set with defiance. "Then, we'll have to just make sure he never reaches the rendezvous point."

Chapter Thirty-Seven

Onboard the Boeing C-17 Globemaster III – Private Airstrip, La Spezia

Andre Dufort paced the aircraft.

It stood at the very end of the grass runway, lined up ready to take off at an instant's notice. Its massive, steel, tail gate was fully down and level with the ground, filling the massive cargo hold with sunlight and a warm breeze.

The elite team of mercenaries wore black uniforms designed for night missions, along with Kevlar vests and helmets. They checked their weapons and waited. The men had been recruited from around the world, each, having served in some of the world's best military special services. There were two US Navy SEALs, one French Groupe d'intervention de la Gendarmerie Nationale (GIGN), one Polish member of GROM, two from the British Special Boat Service, and a member of the Sayeret Matkal of Israel. They were a lethal team, his men, all discharged from their respective services, now loyally serving the highest bidder.

They wore no national flag on their uniforms.

As far as anyone was concerned, these men were stateless – on a mission that no one government would publicly sanction.

The men talked among themselves. It was typical, pre-battle banter. They had all read their target's profile. They knew the man as well as he knew himself – or, in this case – better than he knew himself.

What they couldn't work out was why someone had paid their exorbitant fees.

Naftali, the only previous member of the elite Sayeret Matkal of Israel, was the only one to say what they were all thinking out loud. "I mean, the guy's basically a rich kid with a penchant for archeology."

Edward, a British Special Boat Service member, grinned. "Did you read his service in the US Marines?"

"There wasn't much in it. He trained as a helicopter pilot, toured in Afghanistan, but came back early and had an honorable discharge," Oliver, a Polish member of GROM said. "My guess, his father pulled strings in Washington and had his boy come home unharmed."

Edward shook his head. "No, if Sam Reilly was trying to avoid putting himself in the way of danger, he would have made some very different life choices."

"How so?" Naftali asked.

"Think about it. If you're rich, capable, and keen to avoid getting killed, you wouldn't get involved in half the maritime rescues that Sam Reilly's been involved in. Besides, according to some of these files, he's tougher now than he was after he finished his induction training with the marines."

The lines in Andre's face darkened. He said, "I can tell you from personal experience, the man's dangerous. Some people can be made into fighters, like iron can be forged into a steel blade, but the deadliest are born that way. They have a survival instinct that can't be shaken. Sam Reilly is one of those men."

Dwight, one of the ex-Navy SEALs who had been stationed outside keeping watch, came running up the open tail gate. In his right hand he carried a pair of digital binoculars. "Sam Reilly's got company!"

"Who?" Andre asked.

"I don't know. There's an antique green car sports car. Someone inside it appears to be shooting at him."

Andre's voice hardened. "Is he hit?"

"No. I don't think so." Dwight said, "He's also being pursued by a Mercedes-Benz and also a couple police cars."

Andre stood up. To his men, he said, "You're authorized to kill anyone who comes close to our man."

"Understood," the mercenaries replied in unison.

Andre headed forward toward the cockpit. He opened the door. Two pilots with American flags fixed to their uniforms were slumped dead in the aft section of the cockpit, usually reserved for the flight engineer. Both pilots had execution style bullet wounds to the back of their heads.

The sight made him frown.

It was a necessary evil, but it was a terrible business. The men were doing their duty just as much as he was. More so than he was, they were doing it for their country, whereas he was doing it for the highest bidder.

His pilots – both Russian – looked over their shoulders. "What is it?"

Andre said, "Sam Reilly's got company! Prepare to take off hot!"

Chapter Thirty-Eight

Sam's heart hammered in his chest.

A stray of bullets raked the ground just to his left. He swerved right. Cutting through a gap in the trees, and turning onto the airstrip grounds. It was basically a long straight field, with rows of oak trees lining the outside edge.

The green Montecarlo followed about ten seconds behind.

At the far end of the airstrip, Sam spotted the C17. It had turned around with its nose into the wind, ready for takeoff. Its four Pratt & Whitney F117-PW-100 Turbofans were turning, making a sharp whining sound.

More shots fired.

They landed wide, but were close.

Sam glanced at the aircraft in the distance. It was still another mile away. In a straight line course, he'd outpace the Montecarlo, but he'd make one hell of an easy shot for whoever was trying to kill him.

He swerved to the right again, behind the row of trees and onto a dirt roadway that ran parallel to the airstrip.

He would just have to hug the trees and hope that they could protect him.

He caught a glimpse of Tom's face as he brought the antique around to follow. The man looked incredulous – as though he was still waiting for Sam to give up. Sam brought the Ducati closer to the trees, defiant to the end to make sure that Tom didn't win. Whoever had convinced Tom to betray him, Sam was damned if he was going to let them be victorious.

Sam couldn't believe it.

The only thing he thought he knew for certain was that Tom Bower was meant to have been his best friend since childhood. Even Catarina said that she didn't know who he spent time with these days, but that he was inseparable from a dive buddy he'd had since school. If he could trust anyone, it was supposed to be Tom Bower – but now, one thing was certain, Tom Bower had betrayed him and was now actively trying to kill him before he reached the extraction plane.

He didn't know who was onboard, but so long as Tom was going to try and kill him to prevent reaching the C17 Globemaster III, he was willing to bet his life that whoever was waiting for him onboard was more of a friend than Tom.

Sam opened up the throttle racing along the dirt roadway, leaving a trail of dust in his wake.

Behind him, he heard the growl of the Lancia Montecarlo's engine, complaining about the abuse its driver was inflicting.

Up ahead he heard the wail of Polizia sirens. They were followed by two Alfa Romeos. All were driving hard and straight for him.

Sam cursed.

The Ducati's speedometer showed him flying across the dirt road at ninety miles an hour.

He glanced at the C17 Globemaster III. Its brakes had been released, and the giant bird had commenced rolling forward. Slow at first, but it would pick up speed quickly. An aircraft that size would need every inch of the grass airstrip to get off the ground.

Sam swallowed.

His only hope for salvation was about to take off without him.

Even if they spotted him now, it was too late for them to try and go around for a second pass. He tried to compute a second option. Then he spotted the shots coming from the back of the C17. Its massive tail gate was fully open and soldiers inside were shooting at the police and Alfa Romeos.

He grinned. With attackers chasing him from behind and up ahead, Sam swerved to the left to approach the middle of the airstrip. By his calculations, he would be intercepting the aircraft as it crossed two thirds of the way down the airstrip.

The Montecarlo swerved through the gap in the trees, following him.

The C17 picked up speed.

Sam's ears were filled with a barrage of machinegun fire and the thunderous roar of the aircraft's four Pratt & Whitney Turbofans running at full power.

Dust flew everywhere.

He was too slow. The C17 was going to beat him.

Sam turned diagonally toward the end of the runway.

He pulled back his left foot, throwing the bike into its top gear and fully opened the throttle. The C17 went past him.

Sam leaned slightly to the left and straightened up directly into the C17's trail.

The massive cargo aircraft was still picking up speed.

Sam dipped his head low, and the Ducati crept toward its reported top speed of 169 miles an hour. He gritted his teeth as more shots were fired at him from behind. He kept his eyes glued to the open tail gate, the tip of which glided mere inches off the ground.

The gap closed.

Shots raked his back tire.

A moment later, his front wheel reached the tail gate and he rode up into the C17. At the top of the up-ramp, the Ducati became airborne. Sam locked onto the bike with his knees, gripped the handlebars, and braced for the hard landing. The rear wheel struck the loading bay first; he planted his foot on the rear brake. The front wheel slammed down and he jammed on both brakes, bringing the bike to a stop at the end of the cargo bay, just before the entrance to the cockpit.

The pressure from the ground suddenly pulled up toward him.

Sam felt the suspension in the motorbike depress against the new force. There were no windows along the fuselage, but Sam knew without a doubt that the C17 had left the ground, and was now rising steeply into the air.

He held onto the bike for a couple seconds. The aircraft's angle rose upward in a steep incline.

And the Ducati Diavel began to roll backward.

Sam gripped the brakes and cursed.

He glanced over his shoulder, taking in the empty fuselage at a glance. There was no equipment inside. Nothing tied down. The cargo bay was wide enough to fit an M1 Abrams tank. Empty, it was like a giant slide to the ground rapidly becoming far below. Four soldiers, tethered into safety lines, were at the end of the open tail gate.

His eyes darted toward a cargo net lining the fuselage. It was more than ten feet away. Too far for him to reach.

The Ducati rolled backward.

Sam dropped the bike. It slid all the way out the open tail gate, toward the ground far below. Irrationally, Sam wondered how he was going to explain its loss to Catarina.The thought didn't last long. His second thought was that he would be following the Ducati any second if he didn't do something to avert it.

Spreading himself flat on the steel flooring, he tried to grasp anything he could find. There was nothing but smooth steel.

He tried to jam his fingers into a single opening in the floor – a small hole, designed to attach locking restraints – but it wasn't big enough to grant any real sort of perch to his fingers. Sam gripped it for a few seconds, the angle on board the C17 increased, and he fell quickly.

Like a kid on a slide, he picked up speed, and slipped past the remaining fifty feet of the cargo hold and out the door.

His fingertips scraped along the edge of the tail gate before he fell into the void that now extended more than a thousand feet below.

A hand gripped his, and his freefall was suddenly suspended with a jarring halt that threatened to rip his arm right out of his shoulder socket.

He locked eyes with his benefactor – one of the soldiers who had been secured to the tail gate by a ten-foot tether had jumped out of the aircraft just to save him.

Sam brought his second hand up to strengthen their grip into a two handed one.

Wind raced passed them, dragging them nearly horizontal, as Sam and the soldier, were dragged along in the air behind the C17 Globemaster III about ten feet outside the aircraft. Neither man spoke. The wind pummeled them, making any verbal communication impossible.

Inside, four soldiers pulled in the tether, dragging Sam and his benefactor into the cargo hold. As soon as they were inside, the C17 leveled out, and someone closed the tail gate.

The man who had saved his life shook his hand, "Sam Reilly?"

Sam grinned. "So I'm told."

His benefactor met his eye and made a knowing smile. "My name's Andre Dufort. I work with Interpol, and I'm here to bring you up to speed with the mission."

Chapter Thirty-Nine

Sam shook the stranger's hand. "Thank you. I suppose I owe you my life."

Andre dismissed the praise with a wave of his hand. "It was nothing. I was just lending a helping hand."

Sam smiled at the joke. "All the same, thank you."

"You're welcome."

"Now what?"

Andre said, "You can rest now, Mr. Reilly. We'll be in international air space within a few minutes. They won't be able to touch us there."

"Who's they?"

"The Italian Air Force for starters. Who knows who else wants you dead? We know the Italians are most likely being bribed by the Russian mafia to make sure you didn't get out of Italy alive."

"Why?"

"It's a long story. You want a drink?"

Sam nodded. "Yes please."

"What about food?" Andre asked. "We've got sandwiches. I hope that's okay."

"Sounds great."

Sam found a place to sit midway along the fuselage. It was one of those fold down seats, built into the fuselage. He lowered it and took a seat, keeping his small backpack on his shoulders. One of the other men brought him a bottle of water and a sandwich, without speaking to him.

He took a bite. It was corned beef with cheese, mayo, and mustard. It tasted good. He finished the sandwich in about thirty seconds. Real caveman like. Next to him, Andre took a seat and stretched back into it as though he had all the time in the world.

Sam, his hunger and thirst satiated, finally looked at him. "So what happened?"

Andre ran a glance across him, as if trying to judge where to begin. "You want to know why someone erased your mind?"

Sam leveled his eyes at him. "Yeah, that would be a nice start."

"What do you remember so far?"

"Not much." Sam thought about that for a second. How much did he remember? "I remember my name… there's a few memories from my childhood that pop up – you know, things like sailing with my brother, learning to SCUBA dive, stuff like that – but not much. In some of the memories, I'm not even sure who I am. I don't remember anything about the last decade of my life and I have no idea what the hell I was involved in before this happened."

Andre nodded as though he expected as much. He smiled supportively. "It must be hard. Look, it will get easier. From what I'm told, you recall distant, more permanent memories first, and then the most recent ones. It will take time, but by the sound of things you're a fast learner. Maybe a few days, possibly a couple weeks, but soon enough you'll remember everything."

"That's reassuring." Sam sat forward and crossed his arms. "So what was I involved in?"

"Have you ever heard of a ghost ship?"

"Sure. A ship without any living occupants, lost at sea. Why?"

Andre shook his head. "Not that sort of ghost ship. This is a different sort of ghost ship."

Sam said, "Go on."

"The type of ghost ship you were working on board looked like a rust bucket on the outside, but on the inside, it was a state-of-the-art computer hub, with satellite internet connection."

"For what purpose?"

"Ghost ships have been used by criminal organizations to establish illegal marketplaces on the dark net."

"Why put it on a ship?"

Andre leveled his eyes, as though such a question was ridiculous. "Why? Because on board a ship, the physical location of the illegal website can be hidden. In this case, if things go wrong, the hard drives can be dropped into the sea, leaving investigators with little more than a rusty ship, and some high-tech satellite communications equipment."

Sam thought about the rusty ship he'd seen in the harbor of Vernazza when he woke up. "There was one in the harbor. Is that where I came from?"

"Yes."

"What about the girl?"

Andre's eyes narrowed. "The girl?"

"When I woke up, I was on a row boat with a dead woman. She had been shot. At the time I was certain I was the one to have murdered her. I'm not so sure now. Do you know who she was?"

Andre nodded. "Her name was Zoya Rasputin and she was your connection with the Russian Mafia."

Chapter Forty

Sam let out a deep breath. "What was I doing with the Russian Mafia?"

Andre laughed. "I'm sorry, I keep forgetting we erased your memory. It was a secret US program, something the government doesn't want anyone else to know about. Basically, you offered the Russian Mafia one of the most advanced ghost ships in existence…"

Sam frowned. "And they accepted that?"

"Yeah. It wasn't as clear cut as it sounds. We left clues that suggested the CIA was trying to track down information you had on ghost ship designs, hidden in the dark web for the Russian Mafia to pick up. As a result, the mafia came after you asking for your help – as a private businessman – not the other way around."

"The Russia Mafia approached me?"

Andre nodded. "When you reported it to your connection within the Pentagon, you were requested to accept the project."

None of it made much sense to Sam Reilly, but neither had much else in the previous few days. No reason to start now. So, instead of trying to figure more of it out, he just continued on with the debriefing. "Okay, so I built a ghost ship for the Russian Mafia. What went wrong? How did I end up in Vernazza without any memories?"

Andre made a theatrical sigh. "To be honest… that's a little complicated."

Sam unfolded his hands and placed them by his side. "I've got nowhere else to be."

"All right, all right. I don't have all the details. I'm here as part of an international oversight committee, designed to make certain that intelligence gathering communities around the world, like the CIA, are playing by the rules."

"So far, I don't think anyone is playing by the rules."

A slight grin formed on Andre's lips. "Yeah, you might be right there."

"So what happened?"

"You spent the last six months working with the Russian Mafia."

"In command of the ghost ship?"

"Yes. That's when things went bad."

"Why? In what way?"

Andre said, "The Russian Mafia weren't just using the ghost ship to establish the server for a dark net marketplace…"

"They weren't?"

"No. They were using the ghost ship to hack into secret military networks around the world, including Great Britain, France, Germany, Japan, and of course, the USA. Zoya Rasputin in particular, was a famous hacker, and her job was to pry open the doors that kept the Pentagon's greatest secrets."

"What did she find?" Sam asked.

Andre shook his head. "I don't know, but what I do know is that it wasn't supposed to be found. The Pentagon sent someone to kill Zoya."

"And to erase my memory?"

Andre suppressed a smile. "Hey, that's how you know your government loves you. It would have been much easier just to take out a sanction on your life, but instead, they wiped your memory."

Sam failed to see the humor in it. "Why bother wiping my memory if it was only going to come back?"

"I don't know. Maybe whatever it was you found was only dangerous for forty-eight to seventy-two hours? Once that time passed, it became no longer deadly?"

Seventy-two hours.

Something about those words rang in the back of his mind. He was supposed to be somewhere within seventy-two hours.

Sam said, "What happens in The Hague in seventy-two hours?"

Andre's face turned gray, his lips thinned, and his eyes averted Sam's gaze. "What do you know about The Hague?"

"Nothing. Only that I was supposed to be there for an important meeting within seventy-two hours of landing at Vernazza." He glanced at his watch. "It's now closer to thirty-eight hours. So, what am I supposed to do?"

Andre said, "To be honest, I'm not sure. Our orders were to bring you back to the Pentagon for a debriefing."

"All right," Sam said. "I suppose I'll find out what this is all about when I get there."

"Good man."

Sam said, "One more thing?"

"What is it?"

"How did they erase my memory?"

Andre said, "That one I can answer."

"Go on."

"Have you ever heard about Project MKUltra?"

Sam nodded. "Sure. It was a CIA program in the fifties on mind control."

"That's right. It was the codename given to the CIA mind control program, which included experiments on human subjects that were designed and undertaken by the United States Central Intelligence Agency – and which were, at times, illegal."

"They used drugs to obtain information from spies or something, didn't they?"

"More than that. They experimented on humans to identify and develop drugs and procedures to be used in interrogations in order to weaken the individual and force confessions through mind control. The project was organized through the Office of Scientific Intelligence of the CIA and coordinated with the U.S. Army Biological Warfare Laboratories. The operation was officially sanctioned in 1953, was reduced in scope in 1964, further curtailed in 1967, and recorded to be halted in 1973... and some of its developments, such as mind wiping, are still used today."

Sam shook his head. "I don't believe it."

"What?"

"I still don't understand why you're bringing me back?"

"Sure you do. Despite what you think you know about your government, the fact remains, you're an American, and they want to protect you."

Sam rolled his eyes. "I doubt that. It seems more reasonable for them to ask me to sacrifice my life for the good of the nation, than illegally wipe my memory, don't you think?"

Andre shrugged. "Hey, I'm just the delivery guy."

"So that's it then?" Sam asked. "I'm off to Washington to find out who I am and what I know?"

"Afraid so. Settle back and rest. You deserve it. I think it's meant to be about a ten-hour flight. I'm going to go check on the pilots."

"Okay, thanks." Sam sat up and stopped Andre from leaving. "One more thing you might need to know?"

"Sure, what?"

"It's about Tom Bower."

"What is it?"

"I think he's gone rogue and betrayed me."

Andre's eyes widened. "You're sure? He's meant to be your best friend outside of the Pentagon."

Sam nodded, his ocean blue eyes dark and somber. "Yeah, pretty certain. I contacted him when I found my name on the internet. He told me I was on a secret mission and that I disappeared two days ago. Then he told me to head toward the pick-up point here."

"Which you did." Andre asked, "So where's the betrayal in that?"

Sam swallowed. "There wasn't one. Until about fifteen minutes after I got off the phone, a couple of Russians attacked me. What's more, on my way here, Tom Bower tried to kill me."

Andre's lips thinned and his eyes narrowed. "Okay. I'd better make a phone call. Let the team know back at the Pentagon. Have a rest. God knows you've earned it."

Sam rested back into the canvas seat. His mind numbly listening to the drone of the aircraft's four Pratt & Whitney F117-PW-100 turbofan engines.

The hours came and went. He rested intermittently. Not quite awake. Not quite asleep. His body and mind slowly recharging. There was no telling when he'd get to rest once they had touched down in Washington.

He closed his eyes.

And then opened them again.

Because in the primal part of his brain, he heard a sound that didn't seem to fit the picture. Somewhere up front, he heard the sound of bolts being fed into a weapon.

Chapter Forty-One

Sam stood up.

A single glance at Andre and he knew something had changed. Gone was the Mr. Nice-guy routine, in its place, was something hard and unforgiving. His eyes were like a predator's, hard and piercing.

All bets were off now.

The remaining members of the specialist force moved in from where they had been working in the small cabin behind the cockpit. Sam took them in with a glance. They looked like a deadly unit. Including Andre, they were a team of seven mercenaries, poached from the best elite specialist forces from around the world. Every one of them worshiping the god of power, loyal to the highest bidder instead of country, duty, and honor.

Sam noted none of them had their weapons drawn. They didn't need to. By sheer numbers they held command of the situation. He thought back to the Makarov semiautomatic handgun. There were just two rounds remaining in the chamber. Even if he got lucky, that still left five – which meant he had no chance.

"Where's the tape?" Andre asked, his voice steely.

Sam opened his palms outward. "What tape?"

"You were carrying a secret message on an old Betamax tape."

Sam's lips twisted with wry incredulity. "Ah… that tape. I don't suppose you're going to tell me why I'm carrying that?"

Andre's eyes narrowed. "You don't know what was on the tape?"

"No. As you can imagine, it's pretty hard to find a Betamax player, so all I know is that I was carrying one. You got any ideas?"

"No. To be honest, I don't know why you were carrying one either. Although I have some guesses…"

Sam steepled his fingers. "You want to share them with me?"

"I have no idea what was stored inside, but I assume you want to know why the information was on a Betamax as opposed to any form of data storage used this century?"

"Yeah, it had crossed my mind."

"I'm just the delivery man. You want to know my guess though?"

Sam shrugged. "Sure."

"I assume whatever secret code is stored inside, you were afraid that if you put it on a more traditional storage device that it would be more vulnerable to hacking."

Sam thought about that. "That makes sense. Don't suppose you know what's stored on it?"

"Not a clue. And I don't want to know." Andre's voice was cold and unemotional. "Like I said, I'm just the delivery guy."

Sam nodded. He understood exactly what the man meant. "So, we're not going to Washington, D.C. are we?"

"No."

"Where are you taking me?"

"Russia."

Sam made a heavy sigh. "So, I was involved with the Russian Mafia?"

Andre pulled out a pistol and pointed it at him. "Look, it will be best for all of us if you just sit there, keep your mouth shut, and wait until we arrive. We'll be landing in about fifteen minutes."

"Why? Where are we going? What is this about? Who are you?"

Andre dismissed his questions with the wave of his hand. "Hey. I'm just the delivery guy."

"What? You're just paid to deliver me… like a hitman?"

"Something like that."

"So why keep me alive? Hell, you risked your life to save me from falling to my death during takeoff... why?"

Andre bit his lower lip. "Things have changed. Originally, a price has been on your head since you disappeared from the organization two days ago... that much I wasn't lying about. From what I can tell, someone at the Pentagon sent you to infiltrate the Russian Mafia. Then, two days ago, you up and disappeared. The boss of the Russian Mafia, a guy called Igor Mihailovich – real mean son of a bitch – was pissed off. He put a hefty price on your head. Hell, if I didn't kill you, I guarantee any number of head hunters from around the world would have got to you. But now, all that has changed."

Sam asked, "How so?"

"My contract changed from termination to protection."

Sam grinned. "Wait. You're telling me you were hired to kill me and now you're being paid to save me?"

Andre shrugged. "What can I say? My loyalties are to the highest bidder."

"Who's the new bidder?"

"I don't know his name. But I know he was willing to pay big dollars to make sure you survived."

"All right. So if we're off to see my new benefactor, why all the cloak and daggers..." Sam's eyes drifted down toward Andre's pistol. "Or in this case pistols?"

Andre frowned. "Hey, I don't want to give you the wrong idea here, you're in serious trouble. Your... ah... what did you call him? – benefactor – didn't just save your life to be kind."

"No, I suppose he didn't. So why did he save my life?"

"I don't know. Something to do with the information on that tape. Whatever the hell that means. I hope you've still got the Betamax."

Sam nodded.

There was no point trying to hide it. The tape was stuffed in his backpack. He was trapped in the cargo hold of a military aircraft. They were probably thirty thousand feet up. No way out.

Andre asked, "Where?"

"In the backpack."

"Hand it over."

Sam slipped his arms free of its shoulder straps and handed it to him. Andre opened the bag, confirmed a Betamax tape was inside, and zipped it up immediately. Relief plastered across his face.

"So why not take the tape and kill me now?" Sam suggested.

"Hey, I'm with you… better for you and better for me. But according to the man I work for it's not that simple. He needs to be certain of what you know, and what you don't know. My guess, someone from the Pentagon sent you to infiltrate the Russian Mafia, but what you found there turned out to implicate someone back stateside in some pretty lousy shit. Heads will roll. I mean, some high-ranking Pentagon official or something was about to get screwed. Whoever they are, they have deep pockets, and they've got their fingers in the wrong pie… so they need to know exactly what you recall."

The C17 banked and its nose dipped to commence its descent.

Sam reached for the Makarov.

The mercenaries moved in quickly to disarm him.

His hand never gripped its handle. Instead, he received a blow to his jaw like a sledgehammer, immediately followed up by two sharp jabs into his solar plexus. Whatever muscle memory Sam had been relying on in hand to hand combat was clearly inadequate against previous members of an elite special forces' unit.

He hit the floor and what ensued was a very one-sided brawl. Multiple punches and kicks landed on him, keeping him down low, in a position of submission.

It was a fool's errand. There was no way he could possibly win, but it was the best option he had. After all, he was a dead man as soon as the plane hit the ground. Besides, Andre had just told him he wasn't going to shoot. The man was being paid to keep him alive until they reached the ground – ergo, his best chance of survival was to fight while he was still in the air.

But it had come to nothing.

A couple of the mercenaries pulled him up to his feet.

Sam kept his hands closed tight. His world was spinning. Adrenaline flowed throughout his veins. A unique combination of fear and elation rose as he mustered a stupid grin.

Andre put his pistol away in a side holster. "Let him go…"

The two mercenaries backed away.

The muscles in Andre's face tightened. He balled his hand into a fist. Without saying anything he punched him in the gut once. It was a targeted move designed to incapacitate a person. Short and powerful, with enough force that it ripped the wind out of Sam's lungs.

Sam crunched over into a ball.

The muscles of his diaphragm spasmed.

He tried to breathe, but for a moment nothing happened. Terror rose faster than he could suppress it.

Andre's lips twisted in malevolent pleasure as he watched Sam begin to asphyxiate. "See, I told you that it was best to just sit there with your mouth shut until we arrived, but now we've had to make things hard on everyone – most of all, yourself."

Sam opened his mouth and tried to make a response, but nothing would come out.

Nearly a full minute passed before Sam recovered, started coughing, and eventually took his first breath.

It tasted sweet and delightful.

He whispered something in a crackling, nearly inaudible voice.

Andre said, "I'm sorry, I couldn't hear that... what did you say?"

Sam tried to speak again, but couldn't muster much volume.

Instead he grinned sardonically.

"What the hell is wrong with you?" Andre asked, his eyes narrowed on Sam's closed fist. "What have you got there?"

Sam opened his hand and started to laugh. "You and I... we're both dead men walking."

In his open hand was the pin to a grenade.

The C17 Globemaster III banked to the left.

And the grenade started to roll along the cargo hold with a metallic clanking sound...

Chapter Forty-Two

Everyone dropped to the floor.

The grenade came to rest on the starboard edge of the fuselage, turning the cargo bay into deadly silence.

Sam expelled the last breath in his lungs.

The grenade exploded.

One mercenary was killed instantly.

The blast ripped a hole in the fuselage roughly eight feet wide and sent a shockwave throughout the entire cabin. His ears seemed to echo the blast inside his skull. The noise was followed by silence and the stillness that Sam imagined might come with what could only be considered a pre-death experience.

A moment later, everything changed.

Air whirled as it funneled through the giant hole in the fuselage. The plane rapidly began to depressurize. Two mercenaries closest to the opening were sucked out immediately and Sam, for the second time since boarding the flight, fought to grip something on the floor of the cargo hold to prevent himself from being sucked out the jagged gash in the fuselage.

Air rushed over him. Like an invisible monster from one's nightmares, it pulled him toward the open void and certain death. There wasn't anything any of them could do until the air pressure equalized in the plane.

His fingers dug into the tiny gap in the steel grate that lined the cargo bay. The gap wasn't big enough to accommodate them. The gust of wind raging toward the scarred opening in the fuselage teased at him.

Two more mercenaries, unable to find sufficient perch within the cargo bay, were dragged out the void, with the second one making a sickening crunch when his head struck the remaining piece of steel bulkhead as he flew out the opening, killing him instantly.

It was just the amount of motivation Sam needed to jam his fingers in deeper.

He screamed with pain. It was like someone slowly hitting each of his fingers with a hammer. His legs lifted upward, and his only point of contact with the aircraft were his two middle fingers.

It didn't last long.

The opening was sufficient to allow the cabin pressure to equalize with the outside environment within fifteen seconds.

As it did, Sam found his legs slowly returned to the ground and he was lying flat, his fingers still burning with pain. Sam didn't wait for the next step. He stood up and turned to face his attackers.

About fifteen feet away, Andre looked at him. His face, a mixture of vacant confusion and mulish obstinacy. He was bleeding from his forehead where a piece of loose debris had struck him, and looked partially concussed.

Andre picked up his Glock, narrowed his eyes, and tried to focus it on Sam.

Hanging onto the cargo net, Sam recognized Naftali, the Israeli ex-member of the elite Sayeret Matkal. He'd dropped his Uzi during the original blast. The weapon had slid to the aft of the cargo hold, near the tail gate.

Naftali, recovering faster than Andre, let go of the cargo netting and reached behind into his inner thigh holder for a knife.

Now both men narrowed in on Sam Reilly.

He lifted his hands up.

There was nothing he could do. He was a sitting duck between the two men with their weapons fixed on him – both most likely once elite soldiers. He might get lucky against one, but never two.

Andre said, "Don't move… or I swear to God I'll forfeit my contract fee just to kill you myself!"

Sam swallowed. Took a breath.

In the cockpit, the pilots, struggling to keep control of the aircraft, dipped the nose downward into a steep dive – sending the C17 Globemaster III into a parabolic fall.

For the next 20-30 seconds everything in the plane became weightless.

Chapter Forty-Three

A shot fired.

Sam ducked.

Simultaneously, everyone on board became artificially weightless as the aircraft entered a freefall. The cargo hold was 88 feet long, 18 feet wide, and 12 feet high. It was a big area to be suspended in weightlessness.

Behind him, Andre swore.

The shot went wide of its intended target. Suspended in the vast void of the cargo bay, Andre was now trapped, unable to push off anything to direct his motion anywhere, spinning backward. Disoriented, and unable to remain still long enough to get a fix, he intermittently tried to take potshots at Sam. Naftali drifted aimlessly, floating closer to the wall, and with his hands extended outward he tried to grab at the cargo netting which was just out of reach.

This time, Sam was the first to recover.

In the absence of anything to hold onto on the floor, he kicked off hard, catapulting himself diagonally toward the ceiling.

He hit the ceiling, bracing himself with his hands on a steel girder.

On the opposite end of the cargo bay, Andre – fully suspended in air – rotated clockwise. As he naturally came into view of Sam, he tried to aim the Glock at where he predicted Sam would be when they floated into alignment.

Sam pushed off from the roof with his hands.

Andre squeezed the trigger twice.

The shots struck the top of the fuselage, right where Sam had been an instant previously.

Sam's heart raced as he ricocheted off the wall and kicked to project himself onto the opposite wall. He gripped the cargo netting, keeping himself locked in the one position where he still retained command of his movement if he needed to get out of the way.

Andre took another potshot, but missed completely. He continued shooting until the hammer fell on an empty chamber. Then, without any more rounds, and acting like an angry child, he threw the handgun at Sam.

Naftali finally reached the wall. He gripped the cargo netting, reorienting himself, holding his knife in one hand. He caught Sam's eye. His jaw was set hard and his brown eyes had a curiously malevolent look to them. They said that he was a competent killer. More than that, they said that he enjoyed it, too.

Sam caught his breath.

Naftali bent his legs, preparing to shoot himself toward Sam like a projectile out of a cannon. Sam, trying to react first, pushed himself toward the ceiling.

It was a mistake.

He'd jumped the gun.

Naftali hadn't pushed off yet. Instead, he waited, recalculated Sam's trajectory, and pushed off to meet him at the ceiling at the top of the cargo bay.

Sam had seen what Naftali had done, but now floating through the air, it was impossible for him to do anything about it. He tucked his legs in, and curled like a ball, trying to protect his vital organs.

Both men collided just before they reached the ceiling.

Naftali jabbed at him, but in an artificially weightless environment, it was hard to get any significant force. Sam blocked his arm and gripped his wrist. The two of them became locked, like wrestlers, tumbling around.

Naftali, beneath Sam, slowly maneuvered the knife's blade toward Sam's throat.

It was getting closer.

Sam was strong, but Naftali was stronger. The knife was close and moving closer. Sam locked both his hands against Naftali's wrist. The blade teased the soft skin on the underside of his neck. Another second or two and he would be dead.

The pilots pulled the C17 Globemaster III up from its parabolic fall.

Zero gravity turned sharply into positive 1.8Gs.

The sudden change allowed Sam to twist the knife in the opposite direction, facing Naftali. Sam and Naftali, locked in a violent struggle fell twelve feet to the steel floor. Sam, now in control of the knife, landed on top of the Israeli mercenary. The knife slid effortlessly through the man's 3rd and 4th rib, penetrating his heart, and killing him almost instantaneously.

Andre, now without a weapon, picked up Sam's backpack.

His eyes were wide, his face set with fear and respect. He looked at Sam Reilly. "What sort of man are you?"

Sam withdrew the bloodied knife, his blue eyes cold as the deepest depths of the ocean. He said, "To be honest, I don't really know. But I'm starting to find out that I don't like to die, and I don't think I have any moral objection to violently extracting retribution from those who have harmed me."

Sam and Andre exchanged a glance.

They were on opposite sides of the cargo bay, with the jagged opening in the fuselage somewhere in the middle. Andre's face seemed to have a curious expression. Somewhere between fear and elation was the look of defiant victory.

Their eyes darted to the scar across the fuselage.

Andre gave a cursory glance at the backpack straps on his chest. There were six of them and they were all joined at a single metallic shackle – the kind used by base jumpers.

Sam cursed.

Andre had a parachute and was going to try and make a jump.

Sam didn't wait for him to make a move. He started running toward him. If Andre was in any doubt about his next move, he didn't show it. Instead, Andre gripped Sam's backpack in his hands and ran straight for the opening.

Sam didn't hesitate. He ran toward Andre.

But Andre beat him to the opening and jumped out.

Sam should have stopped.

But, like the Viking Berserkers of long ago, Sam lost all sense of perspective. His mind narrowed and focused, locking in on his one and only purpose. If whatever was on that Betamax tape had caused all his misfortune, he was going to do whatever it took to retrieve it and make the architect of his misery suffer equally painful retribution.

With that thought in mind, Sam followed Andre, and leaped out through the opening into the void five thousand feet below!

Chapter Forty-Four

Sam entered a stable freefall head down position.

Andre, who had more than two seconds head start, was little more than a speck hundreds of feet below him, descending in a stable, belly-to-earth position.

Sam streamlined his body, with his arms flat beside his hips, racing to reach the fastest possible fall rate. In stable, belly-to-earth position, terminal velocity is about 120 miles per hour, stable freefall head down position has a terminal speed of 150 to 180 miles per hour and further minimization of drag by streamlining the body allows for speeds in the vicinity of 300 miles per hour.

A speed that Sam was rapidly approaching.

The force of gravity quickly reached equilibrium with the resistance of air, and Sam stabilized at his terminal velocity.

Below him, Andre, oblivious to Sam's insanity, was still falling in a belly-to-earth position with a terminal velocity of roughly 120 miles per hour, in blithe ignorance.

Sam zoomed in on an intercept course.

He needed to reduce speed or he would smash through Andre, killing both of them in the process. Sam lowered his head and spread his arms, with his legs as far apart as possible, assuming a flat stance. It slowed him immediately, but he was still going too fast.

His greatest fear, even more than colliding into Andre, was that he would go too fast, and miss him altogether.

Sam pointed his feet and toes as much as possible into a flat star position. He completely flattened his torso and tried to keep himself as flat as possible.

The result was like opening a parachute.

His speed reduced to a not so measly rate of 140 miles per hour within seconds. He lined up perfectly with Andre, bent his legs to take some of the pressure out of the jolt – and a moment later, slammed into him.

Andre cried out – startled and terrified.

Sam jammed his hand through the back of Andre's parachute strap, forming a fist on the other side to form a natural lock. Now that he'd made the connection there was no way he was separating from Andre until they reached the ground – dead or alive.

Locked together, wind howled across them.

Andre tried to twist his body and free himself, but Sam had made certain that wasn't going to happen.

With Sam's free hand, he tried to draw the blade he'd taken from Naftali, but in the movement, the knife fell free. In a maddening act of ironic humor, the knife was falling mere feet out of his reach.

Together they continued to free fall.

Andre looked at him, his eyes widened and his face a hardened mess. He snarled, "Are you fucking crazy! There's no way this parachute is going to take both our weights!"

Sam's lips twisted into a sardonic grin. "Then you'd better let go."

"No way."

With his free hand, Sam punched him in the side of his chest.

Andre groaned.

The ground below raced to meet them.

Sam, riding on top of Andre's back, had dominant control of their movement.

Andre struggled, but it was easier for Sam to keep his position. Just a simple fact of physics and airflow.

Below them, Sam took notice of the upcoming landscape. They were going to land somewhere near a large river beside a harbor. A massive fortress dominated the northern bank on its own artificial island, while large Baroque-Style Buildings adorned the southern. Something about the buildings seemed familiar to him, but he couldn't seem to remember why.

Andre said, "We're going to die!"

Sam was indifferent. "Hey, I've been saying that since I woke up this morning... don't worry, it never happens."

Andre brought his knees to his chest trying to alter their position. It was opposite to what Sam was expecting. Sam gripped hard and braced on the wrong side, his efforts causing him to roll over, and under Andre.

For a second, Andre had the upper position.

The ground threatened to greet them at 120 miles an hour. Sam slid his other arm behind the harness, braced for the jolt of his life, and pulled the rip-cord.

The pilot parachute opened, followed by the primary canopy.

Sam felt what he was certain were his arms being ripped free of their joints, but somehow, he remained attached to Andre's harness. Andre's position went from a belly-to-earth position, into a feet first one, with Sam holding onto the side of him.

Their speed instantly slowed to about 40 miles an hour – a reduction, but still fast enough to kill them almost certainly on impact.

The taut suspension lines flapped in the wind as the main canopy dragged against the opposing forces of gravity and air resistance.

The river greeted them.

Sam threw all his weight to the south, causing the canopy to reduce lift in that direction – and leading them to drift toward the southern bank.

Andre snarled, "You fool! We're going to miss the water and die!"

Sam grinned. "One of us is. But it won't be me!"

Sam glanced at the marbled paving that lined the river.

Andre realized what was going to happen and yelled, "No! Please…"

Sam pulled himself up on the harness in a single, hard jolt, and grappled up onto Andre's back.

A split-second later, Andre's body crashed into the marble paving.

Sam's knees landed on Andre's torso simultaneously, Andre's ribs, cartilage, and chest wall all taking the brunt of the impact.

Sam felt all the wind rushing from his lungs.

For a couple seconds he laid there, wondering if he was still alive.

Everything hurt.

That was a good thing, right?

Pain meant he was alive.

Sam rolled over. Andre's blood was spread out across the pavement. Enough of it was there that he didn't need to check that the man was dead.

He glanced up at the sky.

Dusk appeared as though it would arrive sooner than expected, the last of the sun's rays cosseted behind dark grey clouds.

Sam grabbed his own backpack, from Andre's clenched, dead hand – and put it on his back.

A beggar stared at him, his face set with a look of curious incredulity, as though for once, he had seen something genuinely different with his own two eyes.

The beggar's eyes drifted toward Sam. His cracked lips formed a grin. "Bad day?"

Sam met his eye and replied. "You have no idea."

The man glanced at Andre's lifeless body. "What happened to him?"

Sam's lips thinned into a hard line. "Him? I'm afraid we have a firm policy of no stowaways on board our flights."

The beggar opened his mouth, closed it again having thought better about bringing attention to himself, and shook his head. To no one in particular, he said, "Tough airline."

Sam nodded, "You'd better believe it."

Sam leaned down, quickly searched Andre's body and retrieved his cell phone and wallet, placing both in his pockets. He rolled the body a couple feet and dumped it in the river.

Sam glanced up at a large palace. The green-and-white structure was the shape of an elongated rectangle, and its principal façade was wide and tall, with what appeared to be hundreds of arched windows.

He turned to the beggar. "What palace is that?"

The disheveled man looked dumbfounded, as though he were an alien. "That's the Winter Palace…"

Sam swallowed. The man had spoken in Russian and he had understood. Sam had replied in the same language, not perfect, nothing like a native born of the country, but certainly good enough to show that he'd spent a long time speaking the language. "The Winter Palace… where am I?"

The beggar looked at him like he was stupid. "Saint Petersburg, of course."

Chapter Forty-Five

Baltic Sea

Day rolled over into night. The previously bright blue sky transformed into an ocean of blackness. Shimmering stars illuminated the moonless, jet black sky.

A ship rounded Copenhagen and entered the Baltic Sea.

Its dark, sharp-angled and low-lying hull gave the ship a predator like image, as though it was stalking some sort of mythical quarry beneath the sea.

A black Eurocopter AS350 circled overhead, before quickly landing on the ship's helipad, despite the *Tahila* running at over sixty knots.

Tom Bower climbed out while the rotor blades continued to turn, while Genevieve set to shutting down the aircraft.

He stepped out and was greeted by Elise, whose face was set with concern and her intelligent purple eyes were somber.

Tom frowned. "That bad?"

"It's not good," Elise confided.

Tom nodded. "What have you got?"

Elise said, "Satellites have tracked the C17 Globemaster III since it left La Spezia. As we expected, it entered Russian airspace."

"Where was it headed?"

"Saint Petersburg, we think."

"It hasn't landed yet?"

"No. There was an explosion on board. The aircraft lost a lot of altitude, straightened out, rose for a short while, and then plummeted into the Baltic Sea."

Tom's choked down the horror. He was crestfallen. "Sam's dead?" he whispered.

Elise bit her lower lip. "We don't know yet. It just happened a couple minutes ago. Before the aircraft hit the water, local radar stations picked up multiple objects, potentially the size of people falling. Later, some of those objects had recorded canopy openings consistent with the size and shape of parachutes."

Tom's voice was hopeful. "Do we know if Sam Reilly was among them?"

Elise suppressed a smile. "You've been watching too many movies. The satellites were tracking the aircraft, not zooming into the faces of free-falling bodies from it. As for the radar, the quality's exceptional given the distance, but nowhere near good enough to pick up the individual features of human faces."

Tom said, "But it's possible, he survived?"

"Yes. More than that. My guess is that Sam was responsible for the explosion. One thing's for certain, there were a number of people who successfully deployed their parachutes. Four in total. We don't know how many people were on board, but I'd be surprised if an operation like this had more than ten members. It looks like almost half of those survived. I'm pretty confident in those odds that Sam was one of the lucky ones."

The helicopter descended and the black Eurocopter disappeared into *Tahila's* storage hold, removing any appearance of its existence.

Tom and Elise returned to the command center.

Matthew, the ship's skipper met his eye. "You okay, Tom?"

Tom blinked, replying automatically, "Yeah."

"And Genevieve?"

"We're fine." He stood next to Matthew, his jaw locked in defiance. "All right, Matthew, set a course."

"Where exactly?" Matthew asked, before adding, "Elise told us she didn't have an exact location where the C17 hit the water."

Tom shook his head. "We're not heading to the crash site."

"We're not?"

"No."

"Then where are we heading?"

Tom grinned. "Saint Petersburg. That's where Sam will be and it's time for us to go get him."

Chapter Forty-Six

Pentagon, Washington, D.C.

Craig Martin, the director of the CIA watched the secretary of defense throw the phone down, and knew he was in trouble.

Her eyes flashed anger at him. "What the hell went wrong?"

Martin braced for the expected onslaught. "We're not sure, ma'am. Someone hijacked the plane while it was on the tarmac and the SEAL team was away. Presumably, they killed the pilots and took command of our aircraft."

Her eyes narrowed. "And our pilots?"

"We have to assume they were murdered."

She closed her eyes, took a breath, and let that thought sink in. The problem with making a deal with the devil was that eventually, the devil always came to collect. When that happened, people got hurt – and in their line of work, they made plenty of deals with the devil. The question wasn't a matter of whether or not to make the deal, but trying to choose which ones to refuse.

"All right," she said, opening her eyes, ready to do battle again. "And our team on the ground… what happened to them?"

"The SEALs are still alive, although two have non-life-threatening injuries."

"Good. That's something at least."

Martin set his jaw firm. "What are we going to tell the press?"

The secretary of defense looked startled at the concept of accepting ownership of any of their problems. "What about?"

"The C17 we lost."

The secretary stepped closer to him. Keeping her voice low and cold, she said, "You told me it was a wet team, with no links back to our government?"

"It was. But we just lost the Boeing C17."

She shrugged. "Not our problem. It wasn't ours."

The director said, "Sure, but the fact remains the American tax payers are now short a 250-million-dollar aircraft... I'm afraid they're probably going to want that back."

"Then I suggest you find a way to retrieve it."

"That won't be possible, ma'am."

"What are you talking about? It's our damned plane. We have its codes and its inbuilt GPS units must make it pretty hard to hide. So, we send another team in, and retrieve it by force." Her eyes lit with fiery determination. "We're the goddamned United States Defense Force... when a bully picks a fight, we sure as hell don't back down."

"Agreed, ma'am... only in this case, it's impossible."

"Why the hell not?"

"Because about ten minutes ago, there was an explosion on board the C17 somewhere over Russia. The aircraft lost altitude and crashed into the Baltic Sea."

She cursed. "You'd better pray it broke up into a million pieces on impact and there's nothing to tie the aircraft to us, or our ruined careers will be the least of our troubles!"

"Understood, ma'am."

Craig Martin accepted his dismissal.

He returned to his office, picked up a secure line, and called the devil.

Without preamble, Martin said, "You assured me you had this under control!"

Igor Mihailovich was not easily perturbed and never intimidated. The leader of the Russian mafia, he had his dirty fingers in every pie possible. Everyone obeyed his commands. No one gave him any. His voice was slow, confident, and steely. "You told me Sam Reilly could be managed from your side."

"Yeah, well on that score, we made a mistake. You assured me you would fix it. Now I'm told our damned 250-million-dollar aircraft is now sitting on the bottom of the Baltic Sea because of you."

"At least Sam Reilly's dead. Besides, you never said anything to me about making sure your precious aircraft didn't get broken," Igor countered.

Martin's lips curled in delight. His heart raced. "Sam Reilly's dead?"

"He must be. You've seen the radar footage... no chance anyone survived that."

"I was told someone might have parachuted out before it crashed, somewhere over St. Petersburg."

Igor was nonplussed. A senior boss of the Bravta – the Russian Brotherhood – he had connections to the Russian military might. He'd seen the radar footage taken from an array of military bases off the coast of St. Petersburg. "Three landed in the Baltic Sea. The Russian Navy will pick them up. If they find Sam Reilly, they'll know what to do about him."

Martin said, "I was told one landed in St. Petersburg."

"I saw the footage with my own eyes... that parachute fell at nearly forty miles an hour. Whoever was alive there, sure as hell isn't anymore. He must be dead."

Martin said, "That's good. It will make him easier to locate, because last time I checked, dead men couldn't run!"

Igor's voice was filled with curious interest. "You think he's still alive, don't you?"

"Yes, I do."

"Do you think he knows about The Hague?"

"Impossible, right?" Martin swallowed. "I mean, he couldn't possibly have gotten that much of his memory back yet, could he?"

Igor Mihailovich said, "I don't know. It was your idea to erase his memory. Mine was to end his life."

Chapter Forty-Seven

Winter Palace, St. Petersburg

Sam glanced at the Winter Palace.

The building was constructed on a monumental scale intended to reflect the might and power of Imperial Russia. From the palace, the Tsar ruled over one sixth of the Earth's landmass by the end of the 19th century. It was designed by many architects, most notably Bartolomeo Rastrelli, in what came to be known as the Elizabethan Baroque style.

Its architecture triggered something buried in Sam's memory banks.

He was in St. Petersburg… but it was more than that. He knew this place. It was familiar to him. Not just like a tourist might feel having been there, but more like a local, or someone who had spent a significant amount of time there recently.

Sam started to search his new found memory of the place for more information.

St. Petersburg was a Russian port city on the Baltic Sea. It was the imperial capital for two centuries, having been founded in 1703 by Peter the Great, subject of the city's iconic *Bronze Horseman* statue. It remains Russia's cultural center, with venues such as the Mariinsky Theatre hosting opera and ballet, and the State Russian Museum showcasing Russian art, from iconic Orthodox paintings to Kandinsky works.

On 1 September 1914, the name was changed from Saint Petersburg to Petrograd, on 26 January 1924 to Leningrad, and on 1 October 1991 back to its original name. Saint Petersburg is one of the most modern cities of Russia, as well as its cultural capital. The Historic Centre of Saint Petersburg and Related Groups of Monuments constitute a UNESCO World Heritage Site. Saint Petersburg is home to the Hermitage, one of the largest art museums in the world. Many foreign consulates, international corporations, banks and businesses have offices in Saint Petersburg.

None of that mattered.

He thought about the all-important Betamax tape that he was carrying.

What he needed was a local pawn shop – known as a *Lombard* in Russia and Eastern Europe, to hopefully find an antique Betamax player.

Sam closed his eyes, and instantly formed a mental image of the outline of St. Petersburg with all its grand buildings and intricate labyrinth of Venetian canals. He started walking quickly, heading east until he reached a small canal that ran north to south, and turned right. He followed the rich canal.

He passed the Mariinsky Theatre, where the great Russian masters, Tchaikovsky, Mussorgsky, and Rimsky-Korsakov all once performed their debuts. Sam continued south, leaving behind the wealth of St. Petersburg's center, with its palatial monuments and rows of banks, before entering a darker, dingier, strip of town.

Sam reached a smaller, abstract canal, which meandered in a southeasterly direction. The shopfronts appeared to darken, the glistening gold and marble monuments now replaced with high rise government housing. A few people walked the streets, their movements stoic and decisive. Gone were the tourists who wandered. In their place were locals who moved with the purpose of the needy.

He watched a man stop at a dark alley. His eyes furtively darting backward as if to see if he was being followed, before disappearing inside its tenebrous confines.

Sam stopped at the entrance.

He grinned.

There wasn't a shred of doubt now that he'd been to this place before.

It was a Lombard, most likely financed by a local arm of the Russian Bratva – Brotherhood.

Sam bit his lower lip, wondering for a moment whether this was the best place to go. It probably wasn't, but then neither was anywhere else in St. Petersburg, so he may as well take the risk here. Besides, he might just get lucky.

He thought about the concept of a Lombard.

The human race, he recalled, was uniquely capable of adjusting their perspective on sin to achieve their individual goals. The Lombard had been just such a tool since Pope Leo the Great forbade charging interest on loans by Canon Law in 440 A.D.

Since Christian prohibition on profit from money without working made banking sinful, it was discovered that it was not forbidden to take collateral on loans. Pawn shops thus operate on the basis of a contract that fixes in advance the "fine" for not respecting the nominal term of the "interest free" loan, or alternatively, may structure a sale-repurchase by the "borrower," where the interest is implicit in the repurchase price. Similar conventions exist in modern Islamic banking. Various ways around the prohibition were devised, so that the lowly pawnshop contractors could bundle their risk and investment for larger undertakings. Christianity and Judaism generally ban usury, but allow usury toward those outside their faith. Thus, Christians could lend to Jews and vice versa.

The only real necessity for a young man who desired a future in the financial world of the Middle Ages was the ability to read and write; the methods used for bookkeeping were carefully kept within families and slowly spread along trade routes. Therefore, this knowledge was available most readily to Jesuits and Jews, who consequently played a major role in European finance. Later the Jesuits took the role of go-between with heads of state, while the Jews manned the low-end pawnshops. This explained the disproportionately large share of Jews in the goldsmith trade and early diamond market.

Sam opened up his backpack and retrieved the second Makarov pistol. This one was fully loaded. He tucked it into his pocket, mildly concealed by his long shirt.

Feeling better, he stepped into the pawn shop.

A man behind the cashier looked up. For a moment, Sam thought the man's eyes registered recognition, but if they had, the man wasn't going to show it. His eyes darted away furtively.

Sam waited for the man to greet him.

When he didn't, Sam asked in Russian, "I am looking for something very particular."

"Then you've come to the right place…" The cashier made an obsequious grin, and waved his hand toward the back of the shop, pointing out how large his collection of other people's worldly goods was. "As you can see, we possess a great wealth of items. What are you after?"

"A Betamax player."

Sam expected him to ask what that was, but instead, the cashier said, "Right this way… we have three."

Sam arched an eyebrow. "Really?"

"Yes." The cashier, picking up that Sam was an American, said, "You see, when VHS eventually beat Betamax on the global videotape format war, the price of Betamax fell. When they were cheap, some importers, more concerned about the price, brought in Betamax players."

"Betamax lost to DVDs, not VHS?"

"That's right." The cashier picked up the Betamax player. "But, as you can see, some people still have Betamax."

Sam asked the man how much it was and then immediately paid him double.

The man looked at the money and frowned – undecided whether or not he could get away with the stupid foreigner's accounting ability. But the cashier looked wary. "What's the second amount for?"

Sam said, "That's a bribe."

"For what?"

Sam said, "I'd like to plug it into a TV somewhere and watch a tape."

The cashier folded his arms across his chest. "Hey, this isn't that type of establishment."

Sam shook his head. "It's not what you think. It's an old family tape. I want to check whether or not I can see what's on it."

The cashier considered that for a moment, pocketed the money, and then brought Sam to a store-room out the back.

The man looked concerned.

Sam said, "Look, can't I just buy it, use it, and then leave it here for you to keep?"

"You'll pay me the full price?"

Sam nodded. "Sure."

That clinched the deal. The pawn shop guy stood aside. "Be my guest."

Chapter Forty-Eight

Sam plugged the Betamax into the TV connections and inserted the tape.

The video started playing immediately.

It showed himself, with his hands open, in what appeared to be a hospital room.

Sam swallowed and listened to the recorded version of himself – presumably from a few days ago, before he'd lost his memory.

"I bet you're pretty pissed right now. I get it. I would be too.

"You want to know why? Why you would possibly willingly lose your memory? I'd love to tell you, but I can't. I'm sorry. All I can say is that this was the price you had to pay to keep everyone you care about safe.

"Look. Forget about searching for the truth. You're not going to find it, so don't waste your time trying."

Sam bit his lower lip, made a half-grin and then continued.

"All right, let me address the more important things that I can answer…

"How long does it last for?

"Some things are permanent. In fact, some of the greatest neurologists around the world are almost a hundred percent certain that you and I will never get our memories of the past forty-eight hours back.

"Don't worry about it.

"Fact is, you're not missing out on anything. They were pretty lousy. So best that you forget about them…

"Other memories will come back. It just takes time. The human brain's a marvelous machine, but like most computers, we don't really know for certain what will work after you turn it off and back on again.

"When your brain was rebooted, anything could happen. I'm guessing that by now you've recalled simple things like your date of birth, where you grew up, that you like to SCUBA dive. You will eventually meet up with friends, who will also help jog your memory. In time, I like to hope, you'll get your old life back… it was a good one.

"Don't worry. You're not an asshole.

"I know you want to go after the truth. But the truth is, I don't want you to. It will only lead to pain and suffering.

"The best thing you can do me – and remember, I am you – is to forget about this.

"Time will pass, and you'll have your life back.

"Thanks, buddy."

Sam Reilly – the one in the video, turned his gaze across to his shoulder, as though looking at someone off the set of the screen. He nodded. *"I'm almost done."*

He turned his gaze back to the camera. "Look. I have to go. I hope this works. Good luck. Whatever happens, I hope you make a great time out of whatever life you have left. Good luck."

The recording went dead.

Sam frowned. "What the hell was that about?"

Chapter Forty-Nine

Sam rewound the tape and pressed play again.

This time he recorded the whole thing on Andre's cell phone. There was very little more that could be learned from watching it a second time around. He was certain now that the Sam on the tape was himself and not an actor disguised to look like him. The facial mannerisms were too difficult to imitate or reproduce. It also confirmed that the recording had been taken inside what appeared to be an empty hospital ward.

Sam double checked that the tape didn't have any more information on it by fast-forwarding all the way to the end. Then, flipping the tape over, he checked the opposite side, only to find it too was blank.

Certain there was nothing more he could learn from the Betamax tape, Sam left it and the Betamax player, and left the pawn shop without saying goodbye to the cashier.

He headed south toward the Moskovsky railway station.

Sam picked up Andre's cell phone and dialed Catarina's number by memory.

Catarina picked up. "Hello?"

"Catarina!" Sam said, relieved to know that there had been no damage to his short-term memory.

"Thank God!" she said. "I had no idea what happened to you, but our State Media is reporting a large aircraft crash in the Baltic Sea. When I hadn't heard from you, I began to worry…"

Sam stopped her. "Look. I'm okay, but I was betrayed."

"Who by?"

"I'm not certain, but I think it must have been Tom Bower."

"Tom Bower… as in your best friend growing up?"

Sam nodded as he walked. "Yeah. I know, it seems unlikely. But the fact is, plenty of people who were best friends growing up move on with their lives. Maybe Tom and I quarreled?"

"And then, what? He tried to kill you?"

"I know, it seems far-fetched. Of course, I don't remember him at all. I don't suppose you do? What's Tom like? Do you think he might have betrayed me?"

"Unlikely. It's been fifteen years since I last saw him, but you two were always pretty close. Why? What are you thinking?"

"I don't know… I was just thinking that Tom Bower was the only person who knew where I was. Which means he might be my prime suspect. Besides, he took more than a couple shots at me while I was trying to escape Vernazza."

"Tom shot at you?" she said, her voice a mixture of excitement and concern.

Sam stopped, closed his eyes for a second, and reflected on the ride out of Vernazza. "Yeah, he shot at me."

"So, then it's settled. Tom Bower betrayed you."

"Possibly."

"How can you be unsure? If the man took a shot at you, we can both agree he's not on your side."

"I've been giving that some thought. If he'd wanted me dead, surely he would have hit me, don't you think?"

"Maybe. Did he have much time?"

"Yeah, he got a few opportunities."

"But you were on a bike…"

"I know. And Hollywood always likes to have us believe that it's easier to shoot at a moving target than it really is."

Catarina said, "On that subject, how is my bike?"

"Ah…"

"You destroyed my bike, didn't you?"

Sam said, "I'll buy you a new one. I promise."

"All right."

"So, at this stage, there's only one person I know for certain was probably involved in betraying me – Tom Bower."

She sighed heavily. "There's one other person you haven't considered, but you're not going to like it."

"Who?"

Her voice sounded somber. "Me."

Chapter Fifty

Sam said, "What are you talking about?"

"Think about it. I was the first person to see you. You have no idea who I am. I could have called anyone."

"But you said we dated years ago. We were apparently madly in love."

"Sure. We were. In many ways I never stopped loving you. But you don't know that. You don't really know anything about me. You can't be sure."

Sam said, "If I couldn't trust you, you wouldn't be telling me this."

"Or, I'm telling you this because I want you to trust me," she countered.

"So which is it? Are you my friend or my enemy?"

She answered without hesitation. "I'm your friend."

He didn't know whether he was a good judge of character or not, but when he listened to her voice, and the concern in its tone, Sam heard nothing but the concern of a dear friend.

He said, "I believe you. And right now, I need every friend I can find."

"Thank you," she said, relief in her voice. "I wasn't sure how you would take that, but I wanted you to know that I had your best interests at heart."

"Catarina, of course I trust you. Right now, you're the only person I know I can trust."

He then filled her in about what he found on the Betamax tape.

When he was finished, she said, "So what's next?"

"Can you meet me somewhere?"

"Where?"

"The Hague, Netherlands…"

"I thought you said the video showed a recording of you a few days ago making sure that your future self didn't try and work out what happened. Didn't he say for you to leave this alone?" she admonished.

Sam grinned. "Yeah, well I decided not to listen to myself. Instead, I'm going to The Hague to find answers."

"Did you work out what you're supposed to be doing there?"

"No. But the time's running out. So I have to try. I've bought tickets on an overnight train. I'll be in the Netherlands by the morning."

"Okay. I'll book the first flight I can find and will meet you there."

Sam said, "Thank you, Catarina. I mean it; you're the only one I can trust."

"It's all right, I'm happy to help," she said. Her voice was soft, full of warmth and suppressed concern. "Have a safe train trip, and catch up on some rest."

Sam smiled. "I will."

Chapter Fifty-One

The cashier at the pawn shop called a number.

A man picked up immediately. "Yes?"

"I'm sorry to call you on this number, boss – I thought you'd want to know right away."

"What is it?" the man replied.

"He was just here."

"Who?"

"Sam Reilly."

"You're kidding me. What are the chances?"

"That's what I thought."

"Did he recognize you?"

"No."

"Good. What was he doing there?"

The cashier said, "Looking for a Betamax player."

"What did you do?"

"I sold him the only one I have."

"And then he left?"

"No. He paid me double to use it on the premises. Then left without taking the Betamax player."

"Did you see what was on it?"

"Yeah. But there was nothing that appeared to link you to the truth."

"Good."

The cashier asked, "What do you want me to do?"

The man on the other end said, "Nothing. I'm going to find out what happened to Andre Dufort. Then I'm going to make sure the man finishes the job I paid him to do."

Chapter Fifty-Two

Andre's cell phone started to ring.

Sam answered it.

A man on the other end of the line started speaking without preamble. "Holy shit, Andre! What the hell went wrong? First you tell me you killed the guy… and now I hear that there was an explosion on board the C17 and the pilots had to ditch the aircraft into the Baltic Sea!"

Sam grinned. "I'm sorry, sir. I'm going to have to stop you right there… Andre's a little predisposed right now?"

"Where is he?"

Sam grinned. "Right now… he's going for a little swim in the Neva River… but it doesn't look like he's very good at it. He seems to just bob up and down like a dead fish…"

The voice on the other end of the line cursed. "Sam Reilly?"

Sam nodded. "That's what everyone keeps calling me."

"You killed him?"

Sam shrugged, suppressed a grin. "Technically, he jumped out of a perfectly good aircraft without enough parachutes. When he realized his mistake, he kindly offered me his."

"You're not going to get away with this…"

Sam said, "Yeah… I guess you're right. But if you're wrong… well, let's just say I'm going to make sure as hell that you get what's coming your way."

"Listen here, you arrogant fool. We're coming after you, and when we're done, no price will be spared to see you suffer."

Sam grinned. "Then I suggest you try and send someone competent this time."

Chapter Fifty-Three

Warsaw, Poland – Twelve Hours

The train hurtled through the spectacular countryside beyond the window. Sam had the compartment to himself and he was grateful for the space. A uniformed server bent with impeccable politeness.

"May I interest you in anything, sir?"

Sam thought. What did he like? What did he not like? He had no idea.

He smiled. "What's good today?"

The server half-stood. "We just got a shipment of vodka from the Burn."

Sam nodded. "That sounds good."

"How do you take it, sir?"

Sam shrugged. "As it is." He smiled. Judging from the state of his mind, Sam thought the stronger the better. The server's brows rose.

"I'll send out a side of ice, sir."

Sam nodded and the man left.

Sam moved his newspaper and revealed what he'd quickly hidden at the man's arrival.

In his lap rested a Makarov pistol.

It was a gun unlike anything he'd ever seen. It wasn't large, but its compact size and forceful design made it powerful. He tilted it in his hand, remembering how he'd figured out its construction earlier when he'd discovered it in his suitcase. He shook his head.

He didn't know how he took his vodka. But he intrinsically knew that in the gun in his lap the only force holding the slide closed was that of the recoil spring, and that upon firing it the barrel and slide did not have to unlock as they did in locked breech design pistols. He knew that the gun was simple and more accurate than designs using a recoiling, tilting, or articulated barrel. The gun was powerful for its moderate weight and size, and particularly well balanced.

It had been mass produced and was a masterpiece of engineering and interchangeability, a miracle of Soviet tooling, technology, and machinery. Makarov pistol parts seldom break with normal usage, and are easily serviced using few tools.

The only downside was that the design had a threat of firing if dropped by accident, though other than that it was an incredibly safe weapon. When handled properly, the Makarov pistol has excellent security against accidental discharge caused by inadvertent pressure on the trigger. Despite this, the heavy trigger weight in double-action mode decreases first-shot accuracy.

Sam knew that this was not a deterrent, because the men shooting this type of gun were particularly good shots. They often belonged to the Russian mob and as such had been shooting guns for as long as they had been brushing their teeth.

Sam heard footsteps down the hall and replaced the newspaper as the server returned with his vodka. Sam thanked him and took the drink. He waited to sip until the man was out of earshot and made a face. It was strong enough to clean the gun in his lap, but there was an undeniable flavor to it.

He shook his head and as he sipped, he ran over the things he knew for sure.

One: His name was Sam Reilly.

Two: He was supposed to be in The Hague in twelve hours.

Three: This vodka was growing on him.

There was only one problem with any of these three realizations. He didn't know what he was supposed to be doing in The Hague.

Sam pushed his drink to the side and pulled out his phone. The train had wireless connection and he intended to make the most of it.

He pulled up The Hague's website and searched for events that were going on there. They ranged from conferences detailing the situation in Syria, to a talk about the potential effect of solar power on the impoverished in India's slums, to a hearing on War Crimes. He kept searching from different sites, but kept getting the same results. Sam couldn't think of anything he had to do with Syria, India, or War Crimes that had no relation to the United States. He clicked on the link to the War Crimes. An article came up about a recent massacre of Pashtuns taking place by rebels along the Durand Line in Afghanistan, an international 1,400 mile, 17th century border between Pakistan and Afghanistan that remains heavily disputed to this day. The rebels were equipped with modern Russian weaponry, leading to theories the Russians had backed the rebels. This in turn led the American peace keeping forces to mobilize their base another thirty miles west, into the middle of the Durand Line.

Sam grimaced. What the hell did he have to do with Russia and the US? Did he know something about the Durand Line? Did he know something about the Russian Mafia? The problem remained: he didn't know what he WAS involved in.

The name Tom Bower floated in his head.

When he'd called Tom, he had said they'd once been quite close. Sam had no memory of the man, but he was pretty certain he was the man who had betrayed him.

Sam reached for his vodka glass and found it empty. He'd been searching longer than he thought and the vodka had done its work. He glanced around, back to front, and discovered the bathroom toward the front of the compartment, advertised by the universal signage for toilets.

Sam closed out of the internet windows and pocketed his phone. Then he put aside his newspaper and stood up, fighting off the feel of the vodka in his head. He leaned down to put the pistol under the newspaper. Then, on second thought, he lifted his shirt and tucked the pistol in his pants.

Sam slid his way out of the compartment, and avoided death by inches.

He didn't know what had made him duck – some instinct long suppressed, maybe, some faint sound, an unfamiliar smell of grease and gunpowder and cologne. When he'd ducked the bullet that had been aiming for his head pierced the window instead.

Sam spun and got a glimpse of a man in a black coat and balaclava. He didn't think. The same instinct that had saved his life and that made him certain he was supposed to be in The Hague, made him fire off the pistol with insane accuracy at the man pursuing him.

The bullet hit the man's belly and didn't emerge. Blood did though, a dark, wet stain on the thick, black coat.

Sam stood there panting near his empty drink and his crumpled paper, breathing hard in the empty compartment. Were more coming? What about the train employees? Christ. What about the passengers? The last thing he needed was a firefight he didn't know why he was having, and in a train full of innocent civilians.

Sam wiped his face with his gun hand and found his hand completely steady. He readied the gun for another shot, just in case.

And just in time. At the end of the carriage the door opened revealing more men in black.

Sam spun for the doors at the opposite end of the compartment. He raced forward and hurled them open. He passed through them, and then with a grunt slammed them closed.

He pressed himself against the cold steel, panting.

Now what?

A bullet hit the glass inches from his head and he flinched. The glass cracked but didn't break.

Sam stumbled away from the door and stood in the middle, trying not to panic, trying to keep his balance as the car swayed and rocked, hurtling over the Russian countryside.

Where could he go?

The train was a diesel, not electric, good and old fashioned. God bless it. Sam spun and looked for the service ladder and yes – there it was.

Another shot rocked the glass, and Sam lurched forward and grabbed the door. He hurled it open and shoved himself through, into the other car. The ladder would be the last resort then, he thought, as he gripped the gun, glancing around wildly.

Sam raced through the cars, one after the other, toward the back of the train, running past passengers, their screams and cries a blur as they stared after him. Some got to their feet as he shouted at them to get down, to hide, that there were gunmen behind them –

Shots broke glasses and hit walls with metal screeches and seats with muffled thumps, and Sam turned but couldn't risk a shot hitting an innocent bystander.

He didn't have time to count, didn't know how many cars he hurtled through until he opened a door and ran out of track. There was nothing beyond, just a tiny platform and the stretching countryside streaking past.

Sam turned for the ladder up to the roof.

As the cars rocked, he couldn't tell if it was from running feet or the jerk of the track. Sam grabbed the rungs with one hand, pistol held tight in the other, and hauled his way to the roof.

What he would do once he got there… he'd figure that out.

Even though it was summer in Europe the speed of the air rushing past the top of the train stung his face like ice. He staggered, got his balance, and looked back to front.

Then he picked a direction and ran.

He struggled across the slick roof of the train as the men in black emerged from the edge of the train.

The men mounted the roof and stood on it as easily as sailors stand on the deck of a ship. They lowered their weapons and fired.

Sam dodged the bullets desperately as he hurtled across the top of the train back the way he'd come. Now at liberty to fire with no innocents in the way, he shot and shot and shot.

Normally an excellent marksman, his unstable footing threw off his aim, and he wasn't sure he'd scored even one hit before he heard the click of the pistol and knew he was out of ammo.

Shit. More men in black appeared and Sam couldn't even cry. Here he was at the end and he didn't even know how it had begun!

A massive roaring suddenly thundered through the sky.

Sam hung onto his balance and looked up.

A black Eurocopter AS350 hovered and bobbed, flying low, just above the train line.

Chapter Fifty-Four

Tom peered out the window at the silver line of the train under them amid the sprawling green. He clutched a Heckler and Koch MP5 sub machine gun and a Glock 17 handgun while Genevieve manned the controls at the front of the helicopter. She kept her eyes fixed on the train below, flying low. She spoke out of the side of her mouth. "We're getting closer, Tom. This is it."

Tom looked closer, struggling to see through the fog his breath created on the window. It was the right train, the right time table, but he couldn't be sure as the helicopter's speed battled that of the train's.

Tom checked his watch for the hundredth time. This was the schedule they'd seen online. This was the train he was supposed to be on. It had to be. "That's it!" he said. "Bring me down close."

Genevieve pulled the throttle, reducing the gap between the helicopter and the train, carefully.

Tom's eyes narrowed, then widened in shock. "Holy shit!" he shouted. "Is that Sam standing on the roof?"

Genevieve peered closer through the windshield. She squinted, brought the helicopter slightly closer, steadied it out, and then she grinned. "Looks like it. I know he's lost his mind, but honestly, that's a stupid thing to do," she reflected, shaking her head. "Someone's going to get hurt..."

As Genevieve steadied the aircraft, Tom's mouth dropped open.

"Gen!" he shouted. "There are people on that roof!"

She laughed. "Of course, there are!"

She broke off and stared herself. "Oh, shit," she said softly.

Three small black figures leveled even smaller guns on Sam from the previous carriage.

Tom swore as they worked their way aft toward Sam who had run out of space at the back of the carriage.

Sam had one gun. They had three.

The odds weren't good. Tom shook his head and dragged his attention away from the window, waddling forward to join Genevieve in the cockpit. "Genevieve. Do you think you could bring us around to see if we can even the score?"

She didn't even spare him a glance, just slightly adjusted her aim and the helicopter slid lower into the stream thrown up by the train. "I'm already on it, Tom."

As Genevieve took the Eurocopter around to the front of the train Tom resettled himself in his seat near the window. He wrestled open the window and let in the roar of the sky and the engines as Genevieve circled back behind the three men advancing on Sam.

Tom leaned out the window and wedged his gun into the void. He had to hang on hard against the massive force of the air trying to rip it from his hands. Tom squinted and aimed.

Though he squeezed the trigger, he heard nothing, drowned out by the roar of the wind.

One of the black suited men dropped to the roof of the train, slid to the edge with a horrible bumping, and flipped off the edge and out of sight.

Tom grimaced and aimed again.

Another silent puff.

Nothing.

Sam struggled to fire off another shot, and then glanced at his gun. Tom swore. Was it possible his friend was out of ammo?

Tom fired again and the man bucked and buckled and was swept off into oblivion.

Sam glanced at the copter and almost lost his balance.

"Oh, you ass, keep your feet!" Tom shouted out the window. "Not gonna save your life just so you can fall off the god damn train!"

He pulled the trigger.

The third figure splattered and slid off the roof, leaving a smear of red Tom could see even from here.

"Go!" Tom shouted. "Gen, get low, go down!"

Genevieve followed his orders and brought the helicopter to hover directly above the first carriage.

Tom leaned out of the window but he was at the wrong side of the helicopter. There was no way Sam could see him from here.

The tiny figure of Sam spotted the copter – how could he not? – and covered his head with his hands.

Tom groaned and yelled to Genevieve, "Get on the other side! Open the door and get on the other side so he can see!"

The helicopter dipped and slid and by the time Tom could see again all he saw was the top of Sam's head disappearing back down into the carriage.

Tom slapped the window. "Shit."

Genevieve shrugged. "You have to admit – he didn't know we were coming. It does look a little… ominous, considering what he just fought off." She broke off when she saw what Tom was doing. "What are you doing?"

Tom slung his weapon over his neck and around his chest and pushed up his sleeves, making his way to the door at the side of the copter. He grabbed the exit loop and crouched down.

"Get me as low as you can, Gen. I'm going down after him."

She arched an eyebrow. "I'll do my best." She looked at him, directly in his eyes. "Try not to get killed, okay?"

Tom grinned. "Don't worry about me."

Then he gripped the ring and vaulted into space.

Chapter Fifty-Five

Sam flattened himself behind the interchanger, buffeted by the wind from the door.

He clutched his empty pistol, trying to catch his breath. Whoever these bastards who were after him were, they had more firepower than he thought. They'd sent helicopters after him. When the bullets had whizzed by, he'd thanked god the rock and pitch of the train had foiled their aim.

They'd taken out their own men, though? He wondered about that in the deafening roar between the cars. Or was this a second enemy?

Sam glared. A second enemy. Christ. Who the hell were these people?

A clank echoed in the between cars and he grabbed the empty pistol harder. If worse came to worst, he could use it as a club. If he could get the jump on them, that was. He had to keep them close. Closer quarters and surprise. That was the key.

The clanks increased and the door rattled. Sam glanced at it.

It opened.

A massive man entered carrying a sub machine gun and that was all Sam saw before he jumped, smashing the empty pistol into the other man's skull.

"OW!" he shouted. Clutching his temple, the man staggered back. Sam knocked the gun into his jaw and the other man flinched. He glared, and then launched himself at Sam with a roar.

"You bastard!" he shouted. "I'm on your side!"

What?

A trick. Sam could get the truth of that when the gun was out of his hand and his boot was on this bastard's neck.

He rammed his knee into the big man's chest. The wind went out of him with a grunt. His grip on the gun loosened, and Sam knocked it away. In the tiny confines of the car interchange, it didn't go very far.

The big man glared, wheezing. "Right," he said, wiping his face. He nodded at Sam's pistol. "You're out of ammo or you would have shot me by now. You asked for it."

He barreled forward into Sam and Sam hit the shuddering wall of the train with a grunt. He struggled to get his breath back in his lungs as he swung out wildly at the big man's head. The man shouted again. "You idiot! Stop this! We're –"

He dodged another swing. "SAM!" he shouted. "You have to stop this! I'm Tom! It's Tom! You –"

Sam lashed out, hitting Tom in the nose.

He staggered away and Sam rammed into him, knocking him to the decking. He lurched forward, going for the MP5.

He'd almost gotten a grip on it when Tom heaved up from the decking and brought his leg right up in between Sam's.

Sam collapsed, gasping.

"Bitch!" he panted.

Tom grunted as the two men wrestled, weaponless but for fists. Tom got the gun behind him, under him, and refused to budge. Sam tried to shove him off, lure him off, but this bastard was a canny fighter, and strong. Military background, Sam thought distantly. It had to be.

The man got him in a headlock and Sam couldn't shake it.

"You ready to listen to me, you daft bastard?"

Sam struggled to breathe as stars winked around the edges of his vision. He punched as hard as he could at the solid wall that was his attacker.

The world turned black and flickered as Tom withdrew his Glock 17 handgun from his belt.

He pressed it into Sam's temple. "How about that? If I was your enemy I'd shoot you dead right here!" His voice shook and Sam was surprised to hear tears in his voice. "But I'm not." He shook his head. "I'm not your enemy, Sam. I'm your best friend." He kept the gun to Sam's temple as Sam wheezed air back into his lungs, gasping. "We go all the way back to our school days. High school. Remember?" He laughed, suddenly. "We've always fought. And I've always beaten you. Even when we competed at track and field."

Sam grunted.

The pressure around his throat released as Tom pressed the gun harder into his temple. "Do you believe me now?"

Sam gasped, watching the man warily. "It looks like I don't have much of a choice."

Tom stared at him, and then the gun retreated from the side of Sam's skull. "Good," he said, waving it at the small space between the cars. "Then if it's all the same to you, let's get out of here before any more of your friends arrive."

"Get out of here?" Sam wiped his mouth, spitting blood onto the dirty steel. "We're on a moving train. Where exactly do you suggest we go?"

He stalled in surprise at the hand extended to him. After a tense moment he gripped the hand and pulled himself to his feet. Tom grinned and cocked a grin toward the sky.

"Genevieve has the Eurocopter waiting for us."

Chapter Fifty-Six

The Eurocopter banked and Sam was rewarded with his first view of the *Tahila* as she motored along the Baltic Sea in all her glory, like some sort of medieval predator.

Sam smiled. "She's beautiful."

Tom caught his view. "Yeah, you would say that."

Sam bit his lower lip. "What does that mean?"

Tom laughed. "It means, you designed her."

Genevieve landed and Sam re-met the rest of the crew.

He would have liked to spend some more time getting to know, and maybe even trust his old crew again, but he was on a tight schedule. He still needed to reach The Hague and that meant working out what he was supposed to be doing there. So, for now, he would just have to accept that his crew were there for him and could be trusted.

In the mission room, Sam played the recording that he'd taken from the Betamax in front of Elise, Tom, Genevieve, Veyron, and Matthew – in the hope that one of them would see something that he hadn't found.

When it was finished, Sam said, "See… it's pretty weird. So much for leaving any secrets to be revealed."

Elise said, "No. There's something there."

"Really?"

"Yeah. You're doing something with your fingers. They're tapping on your leg."

Sam played back the recording. His fingers were tapping. "I'm probably frightened."

Elise turned to meet his gaze. "I don't think so. There's a pattern there… give me enough time and I'll work it out."

Sam clicked play at the start of the recording again.

He watched it two more times and stopped.

Tom said, "Anyone see anything?"

Sam grinned. "As a matter of fact, I did."

"What did you see?" Elise asked, her voice a mixture of surprise and almost irritation that Sam beat her to it.

"It's a secret code. My brother and I used to use it sometimes to communicate secrets in front of our parents."

"You kept a lot of secrets from your parents?"

Sam shrugged. "I don't know. What's strange is that I remember my brother clearly."

Tom placed a hand on his shoulder. "Do you know…"

"What?" Sam asked. "That my brother's dead? Yes, Catarina told me."

Tom made a sympathetic smile. "We're sorry you had to go through that one again."

Sam said, "It's all right. I figure I must have grieved at the time. It was a long time ago now."

Elise was the first to return to the problem at hand. "How does the code work?"

Sam said, "It links every third letter of the word used when he taps twice."

"So play the recording again and let's write it down."

Sam nodded. Pressed play from the beginning. He slowed the recording down so he could watch each frame. The tapping became more obvious at that speed.

He diligently wrote down every letter.

When it was all finished, Sam said, "I don't get it… this doesn't make any sense… it's just a jumbled mess of letters."

Elise looked at it and grinned. "Yes, it does."

Sam said, "It does?"

"Yes. It's the trail of a data storage site on the internet…"

"But there's no www. thingy…."

"No. That's because this is the code at the back of some sort of cloud computing system…"

Elise brought up Google Docs. Applied the code. And received a redirect to the wrong page. She then brought up Dropbox.

Applied the same code.

And unlocked an online hard drive.

Inside were an array of documents, including satellite images of the Durand Line on the border of Afghanistan and Pakistan.

His mind returned to the news article he'd read about the War Crimes Hearing at The Hague and the recent massacre of Pashtuns within the Durand Line. He didn't read what the International Criminal Court was specifically prosecuting.

Sam skimmed the documents.

There were receipts for AK-47s, M249 light machine guns, and RPGs. Attached were photos of two men shaking hands. One was Craig Martin, director of the CIA, and the other was Igor Mihailovich, the current boss of the Russian Bratva.

At the end of it he stopped.

Sam swore loudly and said, "Quick. We need to get this to The Hague right away!" He checked his watch. "We'd better get moving. We only have twelve hours to go."

"Agreed," Elise said.

In the cockpit, Matthew said, "I heard you. I'm setting a course for the Netherlands."

Sam felt good. He was finally getting somewhere. He'd found answers, and now he was going to extract the ultimate revenge on the person who had betrayed him the most.

Everything was finally going to be okay.

Until his cell phone pinged with a text message. Only, it wasn't his phone. It was Andre's.

Sam opened it.

It was a single picture – of Catarina tied up – and a message...

CALL ME IF YOU WANT THE GIRL TO LIVE.

Chapter Fifty-Seven

Sam pressed the call back number.

"Mr. Reilly. I'd like to start again... I kind of feel like you and I got off on the wrong foot after... you know... you killed my best contract killer – and you know how hard a professional like that is to replace!"

Sam asked, "Who are you?"

"My name is Igor Mihailovich. I work for the Bratva..."

"What do you want?"

"The simplest thing you will ever need to do."

"And what's that?"

"Simply stay away from The Hague for the next twelve hours."

"Then what?"

"We release Catarina. In fact, I'll sweeten the deal. How about I tell you where we're keeping her, and you come get her?"

"Go on... I'm listening."

"We're keeping her at the Ivangorod Fortress. You remember where that is, don't you?"

Strangely enough, Sam did. "All right. If I come and get her, you'll let her go?"

"Sure. It's impossible for you to get there and to The Hague in time."

"Okay. I'm coming. I'll turn around and head to the Ivangorod Fortress. Don't you dare hurt her."

"I won't... that is to say, I won't if you come and get her in time."

"I'm on my way."

Tom said, "You can't negotiate with a terrorist. You can't possibly be thinking about doing what he says, do you?"

Sam set his jaw firm, the lines around his face darkened with determination. "Actually, I've got another idea…"

Chapter Fifty-Eight

Narva River, Russia

The *Tahila* cruised up the Narva River along the Russian border with Estonia. Beyond the windows Sam saw the city of Narva, proud and cold and prosperous. They were running the ship in stealth mode, camouflaged from prying eyes.

At least that's what the crew said. Sam had to take their word for it. To him, it just looked like a ship.

Sam sat in the mission control room surrounded by more high-tech gear and gadgets than he'd ever seen in his life. There was SONAR and all kinds of depth sounding equipment, as well as incredibly sophisticated navigation devices and computers that looked like flat boxes, so unassuming that Sam assumed they had more power than he could fathom.

Amid all this a huge golden retriever minced through the chairs toward Sam, tongue lolling.

Tom laughed. "See? You think you've never been here before, but dogs never lie. Caliburn knows you. Goes straight for you."

Sam reached out a hand and stroked the strong head. "Smart dog. Good judge of character."

Tom glanced at Genevieve and laughed. "Yeah, you have no idea."

A woman sitting behind one of the non-assuming computers tapped furiously at some keys. Her dark hair only seemed to accentuate her exotic, purple eyes. This was Elise, the *Tahila's* tech goddess. She'd been responsible for navigating them to the train on its way to The Hague and she'd been instrumental in getting them back alive.

Tom looked over at her, ruffling the dog's ears. "Hey there, beautiful. How are we doing?"

Elise laughed in disbelief. "Oh! You hear that, Sam? Looks like amnesia's catching."

Tom rolled his eyes, pushing away the dog's enthusiasm. "Oh, stop. Sam, tell them to stop"

Elise tapped some more keys, then pivoted the computer on its turntable so the rest of the crew could see. "All right. Gentlemen. Now. Tell me, who's the best?"

Sam leaned forward. He had to admit. It looked like Elise was the best.

On the screen was a 3D outline of an imposing looking fortress. It looked vaguely familiar. He squinted at it. "What's that?"

"Ivangorod Fortress." Elise gestured at the screen. "Used to be an ancient castle, established in 1492 by Ivan III. Big year in the history of the world, it seems. Now it's a national monument and a Russian museum." She drew on a tablet and zoomed in. It looked even more imposing. "That's where they're keeping her. When they told you to come for her, that's where they'll be waiting."

She glanced at Sam. "They told you to come, right?"

"That's right." Sam nodded, a feeling of inevitability welling up inside him. "They told me to come. At 18:00 hours."

Genevieve checked her watch. "That gives us another two hours. Plenty of time."

Tom craned his neck. "Matthew! How's our arsenal?"

Sam glanced up, startled. "What? No." He glanced around at the crew. "Not you. Just me."

The crew exchanged glances. Then they burst out laughing. Elise shook her head. "Now I know he's lost his mind."

Genevieve took Sam's hand in hers. "Sam, if you think we're letting you in there alone, you really are crazy." Beside her, Tom was nodding and Caliburn's tongue lolled. His tail wagged and licked Sam's hand.

He looked at all of them. "Thank you all for your offers, but I can't ask you to get involved in this. This is my fight."

The mission control room was quiet but for the hum of the machines and the dog's panting and the swish of his tail. It was full of determination.

"Even so." Sam gestured at the screen. "This place is a museum. How is it even possible that they're hiding a prisoner there? Isn't it... I don't know. Open to the public?"

Elise tapped some more keys. Satellite images opened up on the screen. She navigated with some skillful strokes, narrowing in on and enlarging the center of the castle. It looked like a fortress. That was the stronghold in any keep, the most difficult to breach. Elise pointed at it. "The middle section is off limits to tourists. If they do have Catarina – and you're sure they do?"

Sam's jaw tightened. "I'm sure they do."

Elise nodded. "Then that's the best bet at where the mafia men are going to be keeping her."

Tom leaned in, squinting at the map. "Good call, Elise, good work as always. But looking at that map, it looks like there's only the one entrance for tourists." He pointed, and Sam could see he was right. "There, right there at the southern end. Let's say we do go in. Anyone keeping an eye out for Sam would spot us a mile away."

Sam shook his head. "I can't ask you to get involved. I've told you. This is my fight. If you'll just give me back my gun, I'll –"

"Don't be ridiculous," Tom said. Then, turning to Elise, he asked, "Any chance you know another way in?"

Elise grinned. "As a matter of fact, there is... but it's been flooded for centuries."

Chapter Fifty-Nine

Ivangorod Fortress

The river rushed along the bank in a swift moving torrent of pale gray.

On one side was Russia and on the other, Estonia – with the *Tahila* in the middle. The high walls of the fortress gleamed in the evening sun as if the whole castle was made of gold.

Ivangorod Fortress had been established by Ivan III in the fifteenth century as a claim to Muscovy's right to the Baltic Sea. The castle had changed hands numerous times during conflicts and border shifts over the centuries that followed, growing into a full-fledged town as the years marched on. It returned once again to Russian rule after World War II, having outlasted Hitler's disastrous march on the motherland.

The river had always afforded the fortress an extra layer of protection and access. Centuries ago, prisoners had been brought into the dungeon by rowboats through tunnels leading to the outside, which helped deter all thoughts of escape. But over the centuries the river had been dammed, increasing the water level above the entrance and flooding the prison passageways.

Tom zipped up his dry suit. He turned his gaze upward at the live video feed of the castle coming into view in the distance.

It looked enormous from the water level and impregnable in its day.

Sam greeted him. "We'll be approaching the entrance in about five minutes."

Tom nodded. "Okay. Good luck, Sam. We'll see you on the other side."

Sam said, "You'd better."

Tom headed down into the bowels of the *Tahila*, where Veyron was double checking three RS1 Military Grade Sea Scooters known as Ghosts. The underwater diver propulsion vehicles were small, hand-held, electric devices used by SCUBA divers and free-divers for underwater propulsion. They weighed less than twenty pounds each, and had a water bladder, designed to automatically control the diver's buoyancy.

They used a heads-up display revealing GPS that worked on predictions based on its internal mapping and known locations, as well as bathymetric topography – a detailed view of the seabed and seascape ahead utilizing an array of sonar transducers.

Genevieve and Elise were already dressed in dry suits that hugged their figures, revealing both women to be fit and athletic, with clear definition of their muscular frames.

Elise had set up the dive equipment lying out on the floor, a single tank of air, full-faced dive masks, regulators, buoyancy control devices, and fins for each of them. Her head turned upward toward Tom, and said, "Dive gear's checked and ready."

"Thanks, Elise." Tom turned to Genevieve. "How are you doing?"

Genevieve had an array of arms set out on the floor that would be the envy of a small militia or elite team of mercenaries. At a glance, Tom spotted a couple Heckler and Koch MP5 submachineguns, an Israeli Uzi – Elise's signature weapon of choice, which he figured always had more to do with her interest in computer games than actual practicality – a shotgun, and a combination of gas and traditional grenades.

Tom said, "You've been having fun again, haven't you darling?"

Genevieve met his eye, and picked up the SRM Arms Model 1216. "Hey, like Cindy Lauper suggested, girls just want to have fun... grab your weapons..." She turned to Tom and asked, "How do I look?"

Tom grinned.

Genevieve looked beautiful and disturbingly dangerous in equal proportions as she gripped the SRM Arms Model 1216. It was a delayed blow back semi-automatic shotgun with a sixteen round, detachable magazine. Covered in matte black, it looked like something that belonged in Arnold Schwarzenegger's hand when he was the Terminator; not a tall, slim, and wiry woman as intelligent and stunningly beautiful as his girlfriend.

Tom said, "Stunning and lethal in unequal proportions. I'll let you decide which proportion is the bigger one."

Genevieve smiled. "Thank you, Tom… how sweet. You think I'm more deadly than beautiful…"

Elise secured her Uzi to her backpack. "And he would be right, too… no offense, Genevieve, you're plenty beautiful, but you terrify me half to death, and you're on my side."

"Thanks, Elise. So kind."

Tom finished reassembling his Heckler & Koch MP5. He set the safety to on, and attached a full magazine, before tethering the weapon to his Sea Scooter.

Veyron said, "We're there."

"Thanks," Tom said.

Genevieve secured her shotgun. "Let's bring hell to the devil who decided to pick a fight with Sam Reilly."

Tom and Elise grinned. "Agreed."

Tom donned the last of his dive equipment, put the dive mask on and stepped into the dive lockout locker and into the dark, icy waters of the Narva River below.

Tom used his right thumb to depress the speed rate button, and the little propeller began to spin with a whine. The headlight positioned in front of the diving propulsion vehicle flicked its beam off the walls of the tunnel. It was as dark as any cave he had ever explored, but the visibility in the icy waters was exceptionally clear.

The navigation screen suddenly flashed green. It meant the relationship between the current outline of the passageway, based on the sonar reading, had matched with a known section of the map. The two readings became superimposed, and the computer placed an asterisk where it believed he was inside the dungeon's passageway. He grinned. It was a good start. He clicked the route button, and a red line followed a series of tunnels, like a giant maze, beneath the mountain – where the dungeon of the Ivangorod Fortress awaited them.

Chapter Sixty

Outside of the Ivangorod Fortress, Sam shuffled forward in line.

He followed some tourists from Sweden in shorts and button-down shirts. Sam was sweating in his long sleeves but he didn't pull them up and he didn't dare take off the sweater. Under it he was wearing a Kevlar bullet proof vest.

At the end of the line Sam could see a ticket checker in a glassed-in booth. Before it was a man in uniform screening the arriving tourists. Sam inched forward, steeling himself to submit to inspection. He glanced around him. Everything seemed normal. He thought of Catarina and wondered where she was. How she was. He wondered if she knew he would come for her.

He hoped Tom, Elise and Genevieve had gotten in.

A man said, "Next."

Sam jerked out of his reverie. The guard beckoned again. "Sir?"

Sam stepped forward and presented his credit card. "One ticket, please."

The man made the exchange and handed Sam back his card. Sam tucked it in his wallet and his wallet in his pants. As he took the ticket, three men approached from the sidelines with friendly smiles and cold eyes. "Mr. Reilly?" the first said genially.

Sam turned to them, taking a breath and pushing away his fear. Underneath their shirts he saw the outline of guns. "Yes?"

The man touched his hip. "You're to come with us. Special tour."

Sam glanced at the ticket checker, but the man had ducked on to the next in line as if he were scared of the entourage.

"Yes," he said. "Thank you so much. I've been looking forward to it."

Sam's eyes swept the entrance. He spotted Tom, Elise and Genevieve loitering in the wings, admiring tapestries as if they were merely tourists enjoying the spectacle of all the ancient history.

They turned casually and watched Sam being led past the guard and off down the halls. They grinned at each other.

"Show time."

When Sam and his entourage had traveled far enough that their footsteps couldn't be heard, Elise checked her phone. A little light blinked on it, tracking Sam's phone in case they got separated in the labyrinthian interior.

"Okay, folks. Let's hit it."

Sam marched behind the mafia men through the corridors. The halls loomed around them covered with tapestries. As they walked, the corridors grew increasingly dilapidated and the walls became crumbling and damp. Sam kept a sharp eye out and followed in their wake. "Where are we going?" he asked.

Their steps just marched. They didn't answer. Sam watched their backs.

"Not much for talking, are you?"

Still no reply.

They walked until they reached a bolted wooden door with rusted hinges in the crumbling section of the fortress. Though Sam knew he'd be going in alone, the fact that no one knew where he was made his blood cold and hot at the same time.

Not no one, he reminded himself. Tom, Elise, and Genevieve know.

That he didn't know who they were didn't comfort him at all.

Still. There was a certain comfort in being a man with no past. It gave him a certain liberty for what he was about to do. Sam let his morals go. He was a man on a mission, and he gave himself to it completely.

The men in front of him knocked on the door, a series of coded raps. Sam memorized them but knew it was useless. There was no way he could pass the information on to the others. He just hoped they were following close enough to hear. Or that whatever cache of firepower they'd brought with them didn't care about secret codes.

A voice spoke in Russian from behind the door. One of Sam's escorts responded in kind. He smiled at Sam with all of his teeth. There weren't that many. The ones he did have were gold.

Sam smiled back.

The door opened.

He stepped inside, wedged between a massive man built like a wall and a tiny wisp of a girl with a semi-automatic- the same kind of gun Sam had found in his bag on the train to The Hague – just above his spleen.

The light in the room was dim, but Sam could make out old furniture covered in dusty drop cloths, ancient relics tucked out of the way for storage, old power tools, their cords wrapped carelessly around unused bodies. No one had been in here for a long time. It seemed the Russian government suffered the same problem as everywhere else: funds for restoration always took a back seat.

But that wasn't what caught his attention.

What Sam saw was the woman sitting bound and gagged on the chair, the gun trained on her, the way her short hair stuck to her skull with sweat and the fire that still burned in her eyes despite her predicament.

An older looking man with a barrel chest and a mulish grin said, "So good of you to join us, Mr. Reilly."

"I didn't have a choice." Sam recognized the man's voice as the same one he'd spoken to on the cell phone. "Did I, Igor Mihailovich?"

Igor smiled. All bullies liked to be recognized, as though it was a secret to their power.

Sam gestured to Catarina. "Now that I'm here, I suggest you let her go."

Igor nodded. "Yes, that was the deal, no?"

"Yes." Sam kept a level gaze on the men in the room, gauging the distance. He could take out two, he thought. Maybe three. If he was quick and if he took them by surprise.

He couldn't take them all.

The boss shook his head. "What is that phrase you use, you Americans? Ah. Russian Roulette."

Without warning he raised the gun and fired at Catarina.

Sam flinched and screamed.

So did she.

Nothing happened.

Sam's heart pounded in his chest as the gun swung to him.

"Oooh," Igor Mihailovich said. "She was lucky. That time. How about you, Mr. Reilly?"

Sam said, "I don't know anything! I don't know who you are, what I'm doing here!" He felt a gamble coming as the seconds ticked by and he knew they were coming, hoped they were coming... He gestured to Catarina. "I don't even know who she is!"

Mihailovich planted the barrel of his pistol up against Sam's forehead. "Do you feel lucky?"

Sam swallowed. "Not really, to be honest..."

A single shot fired.

Chapter Sixty-One

Sam blinked.

Death seemed less painful than he was expecting.

And a moment later, Mihailovich slumped onto the ground, a large bullet wound in what remained of his head.

The room turned silent, before turning into a cacophony of Russian orders.

Sam threw himself over Catarina, dragging her to an alcove at the side of the room.

Guns blazing, Tom, Genevieve, and Elise stood in the doorway spraying the room with unmerciful fire.

He gathered Catarina to him and hurried her out of the room under the spray of gunfire. It was an all-out firefight and he had to remember to thank his new friends if they didn't get him killed with their rescue mission.

"Go!" he shouted, pushing Catarina into the hall. Tom pushed him out as well. "You too! Up! Get to the roof! We'll cover you!"

Sam had no choice but to obey.

He launched himself into the moldering corridor as cornices fell around him, loosened by the heavy gunfire.

They smashed into damp stone as he and Catarina raced down the hall.

At the end of the hall they turned right, and started to climb the stairwell of a parapet. Elise and Tom and Genevieve clattered up the stairs behind them, covering their escape. They fired off round after round behind them, ricocheting off the stone. The echoes deafened him as they climbed desperately to the top. His legs ached and the graze from the bullet in the old throne room stung like seven kinds of hells.

Tom gestured him forward when he turned back to fight. "GO!"

Russian mafia soldiers hammered up, full of shouting and gunfire.

"This way!" Sam shouted, dragging Catarina to a left passage, but Elise shook her head, grabbed his wrist and hauled him in the opposite direction.

"THIS way! That way is condemned! You bring this kind of gunfire in there and the whole damn place collapses on top of us!"

Sam pelted down the corridor she'd indicated, only to be confronted by more stairs. He hesitated, but Catarina charged straight up, eyes determined, focused.

They careened to the top of the stairs and encountered a door locked with a heavy chain.

Sam bashed at it with the butt of his machine gun, to no avail. He bashed again, desperate. Though the whole place was in disrepair, the hinges rusty and the knobs worn, this chain was bright, untarnished stainless steel. Sam thought it had been put here by restorers who didn't want any unexpected visitors arriving from the roof.

He bashed again, and then spun out of the way with an oath at the shout from behind him. He flattened himself against the wall in the narrow stairwell as Tom shoved forward, leveled his gun at the lock and fired.

The metal shattered with a dull clank and Tom kicked open the ancient door with a violent scream of triumph.

Sam pulled Catarina through the door and out into the hot summer night.

They piled out onto the parapets and stalled.

Genevieve swore.

Before them the magnificent vista of rivers and fields spread in all directions, gilded gold by the setting sun, bathing the world in light thick as blood.

Sam had no time to appreciate it.

There was nowhere to go. The narrow walkway encircled the tower giving no room for them to move around. There was barely even space for the five of them to fit on the wall.

Through the doorway Sam saw hooded bodies flood the scene. They shouted in unintelligible Russian and Estonian, commands and curses as Tom's team's bullets peppered their men. Though they fired off round after round and yes, for the moment, Sam and company held the high ground, there was only so long they could hang on. The problem was they had prepared to fight a small contingent of armed thugs who were expecting Sam Reilly alone – but instead, had stumbled upon the Bratva's strong hold.

Now, like a swarm of angry fire ants, the thugs spread through the passageways to greet them. They would never hold out against such large numbers.

Sam held his breath. He told himself they would just have to hold out as long as they could. But after that… there was nothing they could do. They were as good as dead.

A huge roar descended from the sky.

Sam swiveled up.

The Eurocopter hovered above the turret, beating the air around them into a flurry of wind. Dimly, behind the cockpit windshield, Sam glimpsed Veyron at the controls. He felt a surge of hope. Sam had thought he was an engineer, but it seemed like the crew of the *Tahila* had many surprises up their sleeves.

The helicopter rotated, bringing the opposite side into view.

There, on the side of the sleek helicopter was mounted an M70 Heavy Machinegun and at the helm Matthew the skipper was ready to shoot.

Catarina turned to Sam. "What in the name of…"

Sam didn't let her finish. "Inside!"

They clambered across the helicopter's skid and in through the open doorframe. Wide-eyed, Catarina stared at him. Gunfire spat from the stairwell, past the breached door.

She spun for the rocking helicopter entrance and grabbed on tight.

"All right?" Veyron shouted as Sam heaved his way to the back to make room for everyone else.

"Glad to see you!" Sam shouted back.

"Catarina?" Matthew grinned. "Pleasure to meet you." He actually tipped his hat.

"A little help here, Matthew," Elise shouted, bringing up the rear, and the door slammed shut, trapping everyone inside just as the hoard of mafia men emerged from the roof door and onto the thin parapet.

But as Sam and company had already figured out, there was nowhere for them to go.

Matthew depressed the red trigger and the M70 Heavy Machinegun turned the turret and everyone on top of it to pieces.

Chapter Sixty-Two

Rotterdam The Hague Airport
Ninety Minutes

The chartered private jet – a Cirrus Vision SF50 – landed at Rotterdam, The Hague airport. The pilot taxied the aircraft to the private jet's hanger. A customs officer arrived to stamp their passports and fifteen minutes later, Sam, Tom, Genevieve, and Catarina climbed into a Volvo XC90. Genevieve drove, having mentioned that she'd spent time in The Hague years ago.

Sam said, "Step on it, Genevieve… we're going to be cutting it down to a fine line!"

Genevieve shoved the Volvo into gear, pulled onto the main highway, and placed the accelerator all the way to the floor. "I'm on it."

The Volvo spun around and entered the A4 – where the morning traffic was at a standstill.

Genevieve jammed on the brakes.

Tom swore…

The Volvo came to a complete stop.

Sam said, "Now what do we do?"

Chapter Sixty-Three

International Criminal Court – The Hague

The International Criminal Court was silent, respectful, and somber.

The hearing had been convened to pass judgment on International War Crimes against a rebel general, Saad Rashid – previously of Pakistan – who had allegedly murdered more than a hundred civilian Pashtuns traveling along the neutral region of the Durand Line – at an important navigational pass between Afghanistan and Pakistan.

Saad Rashid, who was currently being held prisoner in Pakistan, was to be hung for Crimes Against Humanity, as soon as a conviction by the international community was achieved. Throughout the entire time, the man had protested his innocence, arguing that he and his men were in the vicinity, but had not been involved in the slaughter.

The chief judge said to the counsel for the U.S. Department of Defense, "If your witness isn't here in the next five minutes, I'm going to be forced to end the proceedings."

The secretary of defense stood up. She took a breath, her lips formed a thin line, and she said, "He will be here."

The clock at the back of the court room ticked by.

The judge said, "I'm sorry, counsel, but I have extended the time as much as possible."

The secretary of defense said, "I understand, Your Honor, but an innocent man is to be executed based on the rulings passed here today. Don't you think it's worth giving my witness the benefit of a little more time."

The judge frowned. "Madam Secretary, you don't need to tell me the severity of my duties in this instance! All right, I will allow another five minutes – and that's it."

At four minutes and fifty-five seconds, the door at the back of the court opened and Sam Reilly entered.

Chapter Sixty-Four

Sam Reilly took his place at the witness stand.

The secretary of defense said, "I believe you have new information regarding the murder of more than a hundred Pashtuns along the Durand Line?"

Sam nodded. "Yes, Madam Secretary."

She arched her eyebrow. "And do you recall how you came about this information?"

Sam grinned. "Yes."

The secretary of defense took a deep breath, her face plastered with relief. "Do you have documented proof that you believe will validate what you say here today?"

Sam said, "I believe so."

She smiled. "Please tell the committee what you know."

Sam said, "I was granted the unique opportunity to work for the Russian Mafia, known as the Bratva, as a skipper on board what is known as a Ghost Ship."

The Secretary said, "Please inform the committee what a Ghost Ship is, Mr. Reilly."

"A Ghost Ship is a particular term that criminal organizations use for a ship that looks dilapidated but is actually a technologically advanced ship inside, often used to serve as the hub for a high-powered internet server, known as a Dark Web."

The judge asked, "And what is the purpose of the Dark Web?"

"To host a secret and highly illegal marketplace."

The Secretary said, "And the Ghost Ship?"

"Its purpose was to provide the physical location of the server, with the ability to regularly move its location, with the added benefit of being able to be sunk in the event that the authorities attempted to board it."

The Secretary continued. "And what was your purpose?"

Sam said, "I provided the most advanced Ghost Ship in existence."

"How did that come about?"

"The Bratva's leading computer hacker, a woman called Zoya Rasputin had sought me out through mutual connections to construct the Ghost Ship."

The Secretary said, "For the record, how did you, a well-respected man in the maritime world, come to work for the Bratva?"

"There was a concern that if I didn't take the job, someone else might… and I could offer a unique insight into the deadly world of the Russian Mafia. It was my hope that I might gather information to possibly shut it down."

The Secretary nodded, happy to keep the fact that she had specifically requested him to spy on the Russians in exchange for American amnesty for Zoya, a permanent secret. Instead, she turned her questioning to Zoya Rasputin. "And the computer hacker, Zoya Rasputin, what was your relationship to her?"

Sam's eyes flashed with anger and loss at the name, but he answered truthfully. "She was my lover. I was trying to get her not just out of Russia, but away from the Bratva – a task that required me to shut down the criminal organization once and for all."

"And that was what motivated you to accept the position?"

Sam nodded. "Yes."

The Secretary paused. She closed her eyes, took a breath, opened them again, and said, "Tell the court what you discovered about the massacre at the Durand Line, while on board the Ghost Ship."

Sam bit his lower lip. What he was about to say would change a lot of lives. Most of all, it was about to ruin the life of the person who had betrayed him the most. Sam said, "The illegal marketplace on board the Dark Web, hosted by the Ghost Ship, allowed criminals from around the world to make deals with each other. One of those deals specifically pertained to the massacre at the Durand Line, with a specific request."

The Secretary said, "Go on."

Sam said, "The request was made by an Avatar – an icon used on internet forums to conceal the true identity of the user – to Igor Mihailovich, the head of the Russian Bratva."

She asked, "What was the request?"

"A large shipment of AK-47s, M249 light machine guns, and RPGs were offered in exchange for the Bratva to organize within its criminal links to Afghanistan, for an attack on Pashtun civilians."

The Secretary persisted, "For what purpose?"

"The Avatar's goal was for an international public outcry, with the subsequent result being that the US peace keeping forces would be obliged to move into the Duran Line, and set up a permanent base."

The Secretary held her breath. "Are you in possession of the Avatar's true identity?"

"Yes, Madam Secretary."

She nodded. "Who, then, are you accusing of being responsible for the deaths of more than a hundred Pashtun civilians?"

Sam lowered his eyes, "Craig Martin, director of the CIA."

Chapter Sixty-Five

When the commotion from the International Criminal Court subsided, Sam was brought out through a secret passageway to avoid the crowd of reporters outside.

Alone with the secretary of defense he said, "It's over now, isn't it?"

She nodded. "It's over."

"And Craig Martin?"

"He's being arrested at his home, as we speak. He will deny everything. It will be a lengthy trial, behind firmly closed doors, but in the end, the evidence you gathered will see him charged. As for Igor Mihailovich… our Russian counterparts are allegedly trying to locate him, although I doubt they will have much luck in that regard."

Sam agreed. "It's unlikely they'll ever find him."

A wry smile formed on her lips. "I see…"

Sam said, "I understand Craig Martin illegally formed an alliance with Igor Mihailovich in order to achieve legal support for placing our base in a strategically important position…"

"Go on…"

Sam said, "Hell, I can even understand how the director might believe that he was doing the right thing by supporting his country. What I don't understand is how he did it without any assistance from the Pentagon…"

The secretary of defense said, "What are you asking me, Mr. Reilly?"

"When you first asked me to spy on the Russians, did you have any idea that my investigation would end up entailing one of our own people? Or was that an unfortunate consequence? Was I an inconvenience to the Pentagon?"

Her jaw was set firm. "What, specifically, are you asking me?"

"Did you intervene in my execution by telling Director Craig Martin that I was too valuable an asset for you to lose?"

She stared at him. Her emerald green eyes an opaque mystery, her lips remaining locked.

Sam continued. "More importantly, did you tell him that you could convince me to have my memory wiped using technology developed during the old CIA Project MKUltra?"

The secretary of defense said, "You know Project MKUltra was a failure and all research was wiped back in 1971?"

It was as much of a confession as Sam was going to get.

The fact was his government needed the base in Afghanistan, directly along the Durand Line. But they never would have received the support of the UN if they had simply taken it by force without international sanction. They needed there to be a humanitarian crisis.

Igor Mihailovich provided that crisis most likely in exchange for US made weapons.

The director of the CIA had made the deal with the devil without formally informing anyone. There was no doubt the Chairman of the Joint Chiefs of Staff, the secretary of defense, and the president of the USA all knew the truth.

Craig Martin, by not officially informing anyone, had maintained a stop gap. A safety net, in case the truth came out. He was going to prison for a long time. But he was doing it for his country. He was wrong. But Sam could respect that.

Sam suppressed a smile. "Madam Secretary…"

"Yes, Mr. Reilly?"

Sam grinned. "Thank you for saving my life."

The secretary of defense said, "You're welcome."

Chapter Sixty-Six

Sea Port, The Hague

Sam Reilly woke up in bed with a jolt.

He was staying in a luxury penthouse overlooking the harbor. A little bit of much needed decadence after seventy-two hours of hell. Lying next to him, still asleep, was Catarina Marcello. She wore a red negligee which hugged her voluptuous figure.

The sight of her filled him with desire, but also with guilt for all the pain he had personally put her through.

He'd finally remembered why he had been so mad at her all those years ago. People, he realized, could be so stupid when they were suffering. They could hurt those whom they loved without ever wanting to.

Sam closed his eyes, his mind drifting back some fifteen years earlier.

It was a time when he and Catarina Marcello had first met. They were at a lookout at the end of Laurel Canyon in Los Angeles.

She was crying.

They both were. He was grieving the loss of his brother, who used to walk up to the lookout to find solace, and she was there to grieve the loss of her lover. The thing that neither of them had known at the time was they had both lost the same person.

Daniel Reilly was his brother.

He was also secretly engaged to Catarina Marcello.

After sitting at the lookout and just staring out into the hills of Hollywood for some time, Sam had started to talk to her.

Neither spoke about their loss. They didn't have to. They just sat and talked.

Strangely, after that they became friends. It was slow at first. They went for walks, lunch, and eventually started dating.

Sam looked very different to his brother, who was tall and skinny. The two barely passed as brothers when they were standing next to each other, so in retrospect, it was easy to see how Catarina had overlooked the connection.

By the time their lives had become deeply entangled and Catarina discovered the truth, she failed to see how she could ever tell Sam.

After all, how do you explain to the man you want to marry, that your first choice had been to marry his brother?

Failing to come up with a solution, Catarina had ignored her past, promising herself that she would one day tell him, when the time was right.

As it was when he was helping Catarina pack for their move, and inside a well-read book – *Faro's Daughter*, by *Georgette Heyer* – a photograph slipped out.

Sam went to put it back and stopped.

His eyes narrowed on the photograph, taken three years earlier. In it, were Catarina and his now deceased brother, Daniel.

There was no way that she could have missed the connection after all these years, which meant that she had been lying to him – all along.

It was the betrayal of the lie that ate at his soul.

When Catarina had returned home, he confronted her about it. She broke down into tears and became inconsolable. It only made Sam angrier. Somehow, in the heat of the moment, words were said that went too far, and both agreed that they could never marry someone they didn't trust.

And just like that, he had left the girl of his dreams.

Sam blinked. He had tears in his eyes. Catarina woke up, rolled over, and kissed him.

She wiped away his tears with her fingers. "What is it?"

Sam said, "I remember why I was so angry at you."

Catarina held her breath. "I'm sorry."

Sam pulled her into his arms tight and kissed her head. "No. I'm sorry I was such a fool. We both loved my brother. It should have made our love for each other stronger. Instead, I let the stupidity that often accompanies one's youth dictate a different path."

She tilted her head up, and gazed into his eyes. "So now what?"

"I don't know. I've spoken to Tom and told him that he's in command of the *Tahila* while I have a vacation and wait for the rest of my memory to return. What are you doing?"

Catarina said, "I have to go to Ubatuba, Brazil for a conference on neurology. It's only two days. I was thinking that maybe you would like to come with me?"

Sam thought about that for a moment.

Before he could respond, she said, "The diving is meant to be pretty spectacular. What do you think?"

Sam said, "I once heard a rumor that the *San Rosa Celeste* ran aground somewhere along the Brazilian coastline."

Catarina arched an eyebrow. "And that is, who exactly?"

"According to legend, it was the crew of the *San Rosa Celeste*, a group of Spanish Conquistadors, who were the last to ever lay eyes on the Golden City of El Dorado. They were heading back to Spain with tales of a city of superfluous gold…"

She met his eye. A wry grin of incredulity forming on her lips. "You want to go hunting for El Dorado?"

Sam grinned. "Yes, but only if you want to come too."

The End

Want more Sam Reilly?

The Last Airship - **Sam Reilly #1**
In 1939 a secret airship departed Nazi Germany in the dark of night filled with some of the most influential people of its time.

Its cargo: a complement of rich Jewish families carrying their most valuable possessions. One such item amongst them was as dangerous as it was priceless.

The airship never reached its destination.

Now its deadly secret is about to be revealed.

The Mahogany Ship - **Sam Reilly #2**
An ancient shipwreck.

A pyramid half a mile below the sea.

And a puzzle that must be solved before it destroys the human race.

Atlantis Stolen - **Sam Reilly #3**
A civilization stolen from the history books.

A billionaire's obsession to unlock its secrets.

A brotherhood determined to hide the truth.

And time is running out.

Rogue Wave - **Sam Reilly #4**
The offer – $20 billion split between four leading scientists on alternative energies to purchase and then squash their research lines, which include the recent discovery of a powerful new energy source capable of replacing mankind's reliance on fossil fuels.

There's no doubt their discovery is worth ten times that much. But will any one of them live if they refuse?

The Cassidy Project - **Sam Reilly #5**

At the height of the cold war, the U.S. military experimented with electromagnetic pulses created by detonating high atmosphere nuclear bombs. The project was code named Starfish Prime. The primary objective was to develop the ability to produce an EMP with enough force to knock out an entire nation's communications.

The secondary objective, along with its consequences, was deemed too important to national security to ever be released.

The Nostradamus Equation - Sam Reilly #6
Dr. Zara Delacroix enlists the help of Sam Reilly to hunt for answers about a book she believes was buried in the Sahara centuries earlier to protect humanity from some great catastrophe.

This ancient manuscript was named The Book of Nostradamus.

The Third Temple - Sam Reilly #7
A mystery wrapped in a myth about the origins of humanity.

A race to find an ancient pyramid hidden in plain sight.

A secret so dangerous its guardians will kill to protect it.

And an ancient covenant that might save the world, or destroy it completely.

The Aleutian Portal - Sam Reilly #8
A Russian cargo ship sinks in the shallow waters of the Bering Strait, and somehow vanishes without a trace.

In the Colorado Plateau Desert, a cowboy follows a river of sand into an undiscovered ruin.

A tunnel-boring operation between the Alaskan and Siberian peninsulas is stalled when its largest burrowing machine disappears into an abyss.

Code to Extinction - Sam Reilly #9

A tempestuous mass of dark, foreboding sky seems to be spreading across the globe.

In Arizona, an astronomer tries to decipher the hidden message inside a thirteen-thousand-year-old megalithic stone, which just might hold the key to everything.

Can Sam Reilly and his unique team break the Code to Extinction?

The Ironclad Covenant - **Sam Reilly #10**

On May 18th, 1863 – the day the siege of the Confederate stronghold at Vicksburg began – a secret war chest was removed by an ironclad and taken away along the Mississippi River.

It contained a Covenant capable of altering the entire course of the Civil War. Its destination was Washington, D.C.

A place it never reached.

The Heisenberg Legacy – **Sam Reilly #11**

On January the 22nd, 1945, a secret weapon of unimaginable power was brought from the quiet town of Haigerloch in Germany's southwest, and loaded onto a plane waiting at Stuttgart.

Less than a dozen people knew of the weapon's existence, and even less knew where it was being taken.

The aircraft, its crew, and its remarkable cargo were never seen again.

Until now.

Omega Deep – **Sam Reilly #12**

The US Navy's most advanced nuclear attack submarine, the *USS Omega Deep* was the first to disappear.

It was followed swiftly by the loss of the Russian spy vessel *Vostok*, and then the *Feng Jian*, a Chinese Aircraft Carrier.

Sam Reilly and his unique team of troubleshooters are requested at the express order of the President of the United States of America to locate the *Omega Deep* and determine the cause of these unexplained tragedies, before they lead to World War III.

The Holy Grail – Sam Reilly #13
When a panicked man with purple eyes grabs Sam at gunpoint and takes him hostage, Sam knows that this is more than a mere ransom opportunity; this man is scared of something...

And Sam is going to have to find what it is if he wants to stay alive.

The Phoenix Sanction – Sam Reilly #14
On board Phoenix Airlines Flight 318, Andrew Goddard awakens to discover the cockpit empty and all the passengers unconscious.

In the Colorado Monarch Mountains, an old gold miner discovers a fiendish stone mask sealed inside an obsidian chamber.

Sam Reilly has just three weeks to find out how the two unlikely events are connected, and the secret behind it might change everything we thought we knew about humanity.

Habitat Zero – Sam Reilly #15
In the Pacific Ocean, a Silicon Valley magnate vacationing on his luxury motor yacht *Carpe Diem*, stumbles across a floating island of pumice.

Two weeks later, the motor yacht returns to its home port in San Diego on autopilot – but when it arrives, nobody disembarks.

Sam Reilly and his team are called in to investigate what happened on board *Carpe Diem*. But what at first appears to be a simple boating accident soon turns into a deadly game of international intrigue – sending America and Russia racing toward each other on an unavoidable collision course.

The Hunt for Excalibur – Sam Reilly #16

On March 11, 2011, the Japanese fishing trawler, *Hoshi Maru* accidentally hauled up something deadly into its live-fish hold. The crew, having discovered their mistake, raced toward the harbor in the hope that they might survive.

They never made it.

Sam Reilly will need to discover what really happened on board the *Hoshi Maru* – and why all clues point to the Legend of King Arthur.

Ghost Ship – Sam Reilly #17

In the dead of night, a decrepit, unmarked motor yacht drifts into the medieval port of Vernazza, Italy.

Less than fifty yards away, a man wakes up on board a small rowboat, covered in blood.

The man asks himself one question: Who am I?

The Tomb of El Dorado – Sam Reilly #18

A city cloaked in legend too fanciful to be true.

An ancient tribe, who have vowed to protect their Gods until the end of time.

A shipwreck scattered with gold, and drawings of a mythical beast.

Sam Reilly is on the hunt to find an ancient tomb, before El Dorado is lost forever...

Made in the USA
Columbia, SC
12 May 2020

96712314R00143